THE BOOK
OF ANNA

THE BOOK OF ANNA

(Karenina's Novel)

Carmen Boullosa

Translated by Samantha Schnee

COFFEE HOUSE PRESS
Minneapolis
2020

First published in Spanish as *El libro de Ana* by
Ediciones Siruela (Madrid) and Alfaguara (Mexico City)

Coffee House Press books are available to the trade through our primary distributor, Consortium Book Sales & Distribution, cbsd.com or (800) 283-3572. For personal orders, catalogs, or other information, write to info@coffeehousepress.org.

Coffee House Press is a nonprofit literary publishing house. Support from private foundations, corporate giving programs, government programs, and generous individuals helps make the publication of our books possible. We gratefully acknowledge their support in detail in the back of this book.

LIBRARY OF CONGRESS CATALOGING-IN-PUBLICATION DATA

Names: Boullosa, Carmen, author. | Schnee, Samantha, translator.
Title: The book of Anna : (Karenina's novel) / Carmen Boullosa ;
    translated by Samantha Schnee.
Other titles: Libro de Ana. English
Description: First English-language edition. | Minneapolis : Coffee
    House Press, 2020. | First published in Spanish as El libro de Ana
    (Ediciones Siruela and Alfaguara, 2016)
Identifiers: LCCN 2019028600 (print) | LCCN 2019028601 (ebook) |
    ISBN 9781566895774 (trade paperback) | ISBN 9781566895859 (ebook)
Subjects: LCSH: Soviet Union—History—Revolution, 1917-1921—
    Fiction. | GSAFD: Alternative histories (Fiction)
Classification: LCC PQ7298.12.O76 L4313 2020 (print) |
    LCC PQ7298.12.O76 (ebook) | DDC 863/.64—dc23
LC record available at https://lccn.loc.gov/2019028600
LC ebook record available at https://lccn.loc.gov/2019028601

PRINTED IN THE UNITED STATES OF AMERICA
27 26 25 24 23 22 21 20   1 2 3 4 5 6 7 8

"Tell me the truth: why does the woman in your short story kill herself?"

"Oh! You'd have to ask her."

"And *you* can't do that?"

"That's as impossible as asking a question of an image in a dream."

—FELISBERTO HERNÁNDEZ

On the road to redemption,
light doesn't cease throbbing.
I believe in love because I'm never satisfied.
It's my wild heart
that arrives in the nick of time.

—GUSTAVO CERATI

Any woman who spent her whole life with Tolstoy certainly deserves a good measure of sympathy.

—SUSAN JACOBY

Her occupations are, firstly, writing. . . . She is writing a children's book and does not speak of it to anyone, but she read it to me and I showed the manuscript to Vorkuyev. . . . You know, the publisher. . . . He is an expert, and says it is a remarkable work.

...

She rose and took up a book bound in morocco-leather.

"Let me have it, Anna Arkadyevna," said Vorkuyev, pointing to the book. "It is well worth it."

"Oh no, it is so unfinished!"

—LEO TOLSTOY,
Anna Karenina (Part 7, Chapters IX–X)
Translated by Louise and Aylmer Maude, 1918

CONTENTS

PART TWO: BLOODY SUNDAY
Sunday, January 9, 1905

PART THREE: KARENINA'S PORTRAIT
Three months later

PART FOUR: THE BOOK OF ANNA
No date or place

PART FIVE: FINALE
St. Petersburg, June 1905

An Explanation of What This Book Is About

In his novel *Anna Karenina*, Tolstoy tells us that his lead character authored a book of the highest quality. Vorkuyev, a publisher, tells her he wants to print it. ("Let me have it, Anna Arkadyevna. . . . It is well worth it.") But Anna considers it a draft. ("Oh no, it is so unfinished!")

After this passage, Tolstoy never mentions Anna's book again.

What he doesn't tell us is that Karenina continues to work on her manuscript. The few mornings she's in the right state of mind, she begins making minor corrections. Then it becomes her companion at all hours, even in her opium-filled nights. Eventually she rewrites it from beginning to end.

Anna left two books, then: the one her contemporaries knew about, and the one that was with her to the end. The night before her fall she was still rewriting it.

This is the story of how Karenina's revised version—presented here for the first time—was rescued from oblivion, in 1905, in St. Petersburg, at the dawn of the Russian Revolution.

PART ONE

ANNA'S SERGEI AND ANYA'S CITY

St. Petersburg, Saturday, January 8, 1905

I. On the Heels of Clementine, the Anarchist

A stone's throw from the majestic avenue known as Nevsky Prospekt, handsome Clementine hurries along, wrapped in a cloak that, in her haste, has slipped down to reveal a glimpse of her pink dress and something she's carrying in her arms. She notices a vigilant gendarme and slows down as she approaches him, changing her demeanor, whispering a lullaby, "sh-sh-sh-sh." The policeman hears her but doesn't look over, there are so many poor souls carrying around babes in arms, these women mean nothing to him. He's under orders to keep a strict watch, and that doesn't include meddling in the affairs of starving mothers.

Clementine's head is covered by a garment she's cut and sewn with her own hands; it protects her neck and matches her striking cape, made from the scraps of different pelts. She pauses to glance at a poorly produced notice; the printers have joined the strike too: "It is forbidden to gather in the streets with intent to disturb the peace, upon pain of death."

She hastens along, thinking, *They've just posted it!* And then, *This doesn't bode well, not well at all!* She picks up her pace.

She arrives at the kiosk of the tram that crosses the frozen Neva. She asks for a round-trip ticket.

"It's the last run of the day, ma'am, it's going out and coming right back."

Clementine hesitates.

"Don't waste my time, ma'am. Round trip?"

"Can I use the other half of the ticket later?"

"Of course!"

"It's cheaper if I buy a round trip?"

"Why're you asking if you already know?"

"Then give me a round trip."

Clementine walks down the jetty repeating "sh-sh-sh," her lullaby; she hands half her ticket to the young man standing at the door of the tram, boards, and takes the last seat on the right. The driver (and ticket salesman) boards last. The young man standing at the door of the tram shouts, "See you tomorrow!" The tram begins to move.

They cross over the Neva and stop at the mouth of one of the river's tributaries, at the Alexander jetty. The passengers get off, except Clementine. The driver glances at her out of the corner of his eye, impatiently. Since Clementine hasn't budged, he turns to look at her, hands on his hips. Without moving from her seat, Clementine, bundled in her cloak, says:

"I'm not getting off. I forgot something, I have to go back."

"Women!" mutters the driver. "Ma'am, these are no times to be throwing money away! Especially not for people such as yourself! What a waste. . . . Think of your child, ma'am!"

Clementine nods, with an aggrieved expression.

"You're absolutely right."

The driver repeats:

"I told you, there are no more runs today, this is the last one."

"What else can I do? I have to go back. Here, take my ticket!" Clementine moves as if to get out of her seat. The driver declines, waving both hands.

"Don't give me a thing. Let's just pretend you didn't take this trip, don't get off. . . ."

"I wasn't going to."

"Don't open your mouth, ma'am, don't say another word, don't test my patience. Just stay put."

Grumbling who knows what between gritted teeth, the man adjusts the collar of his coat and steps off this old workers' tram. He closes the door behind him.

Clementine settles in her seat. She shudders with nerves; she tries to shake them off. Beneath her cape she removes something from the bundle in her arms—the one she's been carrying like a baby. It's a homemade bomb. She carefully slides it down her torso, past her hips, her right leg, setting it gently beneath her seat, in between her feet. She stays hunched over, hiding the bomb with her cloak.

The driver opens the tram door and steps into his compartment, where he checks the tickets of the passengers as they board one by one until the tram is full. They set off.

They return to the jetty on the south bank of the river. The moment they arrive, the passengers rush to get off. Clementine leans over farther, remaining in her seat. Her hands beneath her cloak, she pulls the fuse of the bomb and pushes it to the back corner of the tram. She rises, adjusts her cloak, and, pretending to embrace what remains of her dummy babe, gets off the tram, the last passenger to disembark. The driver closes the tram door, and, striding briskly past her, he leaves the jetty, heading east.

The wind is ferocious, carrying sharp blades of snow. Clementine walks westward, each step longer than the last. As she moves farther away from the jetty, her expression changes from one of self-satisfied cunning to the anxiety of flight. She presses ahead, resisting the impulse to look back, listening closely. Her demeanor continues to change: from anxiety to fear, from fear to excitement, to impatience, to despair, to anger.

"Nothing!" she mutters. "It didn't explode! What hopeless idiots we are! It was supposed to explode in sixty seconds, it's already been . . ." She doesn't finish her sentence, filled with rage. She raises the bundle in her arms (the dummy babe) to her neck, pulling her cloak around her. She continues walking. From the direction of the jetty, she hears a faint noise. Like an old man farting—the drawn-out, muffled sound of malfunction—it's an absurd explosion, nothing like the burst of gunpowder Clementine hoped to hear and that would have blown the tram and the jetty to smithereens, splintering the rails and the frozen Neva. No one will rush to see what the noise was.

An interminable moment later, she hears something that can't be described as even a tiny explosion, like the sound of a rag doll falling from a shelf. Clementine leaves the vicinity of the river with long, hurried strides, her expression one of wild-eyed despair. Out of the corner of her eye, she sees the notice that caught her attention, the one forbidding demonstrations. Again she sees the gendarme who heard her hushing her pretend child, and again she whispers "sh-sh-sh" as she passes by him steadily; she doesn't break into a run. A few steps later, she changes her "sh-sh-sh" to a popular tune. She pauses. *That good-for-nothing bomb will be the end of me!* she thinks, and she picks up her pace.

2. Claudia and Sergei

Claudia enters the dining room with short, quick steps, shaking her skirt with one hand. As she walks, her smiling gaze flits across the room, from a piece of furniture, to an object, to another, playfully, without stopping. She comes to a halt, settles her gaze on Sergei for a few moments, and says:

"What's all the commotion?"

In this household they breathe happiness; it's everywhere you look. The dining room, arranged with the same care as the rest of the home, is comfortable and charming. But Sergei is sitting at the table, looking pained. His movements are tense; he's on tenterhooks. He responds to Claudia's sweet gaze by nearly jumping out of his chair, catlike, scowling angrily in ill-tempered silence.

"All right, all right," Claudia says, trying to calm him. "It is what it is, it was what it was; as they say, forget about it."

She notices a streak of flour on her skirt, tries to brush it off, and says offhandedly:

"We need to leave promptly at seven, on the dot."

Sergei hasn't heard a word since she asked him what the commotion was. *Why am I so worried?* The question echoes in his head. *So worried, so worried.* He lets this thought repeat three or four times and replies violently, "Claudine, you don't seem to understand: I'm not upset. Good God! Consider one simple thing: The scandal. The scandal! I won't be able to bear it. But I can't say no. . . . The request comes straight from the tsar's desk. . . . I can already see myself in chains on the Solovetsky Islands. . . . I'd rather have the shackles than the scandal!"

"The Solovetsky Islands! Don't be ridiculous! We're not living in the times of Ivan the Terrible."

"They're worse than that! I'll face opprobrium, and . . . !"

"Sergei, Sergei, calm down, Sergei . . ."

"Even worse!"

"We're going to dress formally and leave at 7:10 on the dot, like the English." She's changed the time of departure; it doesn't matter to her, and Sergei, wrapped up in his own world, doesn't notice.

"The scandal! I can't anger the tsar. . . . But if I accept: The scandal! I can't bear it."

"What scandal? There's nothing scandalous about behaving like the English. Well, there's Afghanistan. . . ." She refrains from the tirade she's about to deliver to Sergei because she realizes what he's just said. "Anger the tsar? Why would he be angry with you?" She barely manages to stop herself from saying it in time; she knows her husband would explode, and she closes her eyes so they don't betray her. "Don't even think about rejecting his request!"

"Behaving like the English? What on earth are you talking about, Claudine? You can't listen to what I'm saying for more than two minutes?"

"Sergei, my love," she feigns patience; the softness of her voice infuriates Sergei.

"Don't start with your 'my loves.' Don't you dare 'my love' me!" He's livid. He doesn't have outbursts like this with anyone except his wife.

"I don't know what to do with you, Sergei. Sergei, Sergei," Claudia lets her soft gaze rest on him, but he doesn't notice because he's staring out the window. He breathes deeply; he wants to calm down. He's so angry, he can't see a thing. Claudia lets her gaze follow his out the window, where bright snow falls like tiny diamonds. "Sergei, Sergei," she keeps repeating, without paying him any attention, enjoying the silent dazzle of the flakes.

Before she finishes her rosary of *Sergeis*, he mutters, voice still choked by anger, jaw set, hands in fists, "It's not *my* problem. . . . Don't you see? Don't you realize?" And he adds, as if to himself, "You can't, because you're so stubborn, or unfeeling. Like the English! How could you say such a thing? It's the last straw!"

Claudia doesn't hear the rest. The joy of seeing the light refracted in the snow is like an electric charge: intense, lightning quick, and uncomfortable, too, because of its inopportune timing.

In less time than it takes to describe this sensation, Claudia has moved on, slipped out into the kitchen, where she knows she should return.

The yeast that has been in her family for generations has turned a strange color, which worries the cook, Lantur (who knows where her name comes from). Lantur had shown "Young Claudia" the tray of dough, waving her flour-covered hands and dirtying Claudia's dress. Lantur expected Claudia to respond as she usually did, dismissing her concerns, saying, "It's nothing, Lantur, nothing, back to work!" But instead Claudia's expression had changed when she looked at the dough, and though she tried to compose herself ("I'm going to look in on Sergei, I'll be right back"), when she rushed out as quickly as she had rushed in, it was clear that the dough boded ill: "Now we're in trouble."

After trying to comfort her husband, Claudia returns to the kitchen. The cook, who is distressed—but protective of her work—is still standing where Claudia left her, passing the tray of dough from one hand to the other. Claudia pokes the dough with her index fingers. It feels even worse than it looks: "It's certainly off," she says, but since she's got Sergei raging in the room next door, she issues a command. "Give it a try, Lantur, make the bread just as you always do, let's hope it bakes well," and she retraces her steps, unaware that she says aloud, "Is the world coming to an end?"

"It's not the end of anything," Sergei replies angrily. "It's just starting. I don't see how to avoid it. . . . Help me think, Claudine. . . . For God's sake! Be still!"

Claudia faces him. She looks at him—hands raised, palms outward, index fingers, still feeling the strange consistency of the dough, extended to keep from dirtying her clothes—and when she realizes the position her fingers are in, she extends her arms toward Sergei and says playfully, "Olé, torero! Olé! Watch my horns, here!"

As a girl, she had been to a bullfight on one of the many trips she took with her father, the ambassador, a good-natured, light-hearted man who knew how to enjoy everything life had to offer and took great pride in his busy diplomatic engagements, sometimes saying, "My wife and I don't remember clearly where our children were born, they were all born in different places." It was true: her mother confused her pregnancies and their births, and for him it was all one big party. Eleven children born in eleven different cities—their parents confused their birth years, even their names.

Claudia is their eighth child. She and her siblings were named after the countries in which they were born, "To aid my memory," her mother used to say, "not that it helps much!" Ten boys and one girl, little Claudia, who was born in Spain.

Sergei looks at his wife pretending to charge at him and takes her joke as an attack; he's still wrapped up in his own world. "I'm sunk, there's no way out of this mess. It's the end. I'm a dead man. I can't go on."

"Listen to me, Sergei. I know what you're thinking. What a face! You look like you're fighting in Japan and you've lost your men! Wipe that look off your face. You're sinking in a glass of water. Not another word about the tsar's letter until we've returned from the theater. Because I really, really, *really* want to go to the New Year's concert. And I want to go for you, you've been looking forward to this for days. Enough! All right? When we get home we'll decide what to say and what to do. But let it go for the time being, think about something else. . . . Stop tormenting yourself. Enough."

"There's nothing to say, Claudine, I'm done for. . . . Calling the tsar a *glass of water!*"

"Stop, stop!" sweet, patient Claudia says. "Take a deep breath!"

Claudia was marked by the sun of Seville. Her mother gave birth to her there at midday. Between one step and the next, she felt an intense cramping, the little girl appeared before she even had time to squat down, the midwife had to catch the baby to save her from hitting the floor. The couple's entourage fell over themselves looking after the ambassador's wife, and despite the fact that she didn't need to rest (she could have walked anywhere she needed to go), they wouldn't let her take a step.

"But I'm fine! Nothing's wrong!"

"Don't lift a finger!" the ambassador replied, untroubled, unashamed, unembarrassed. That's how easily his wife gave birth: she didn't even know when her babies were about to be born. Her fertility filled him with pride. Overjoyed with his little girl (his first), when he held her he practically shouted, "Vivo Sevilla! Viva Sevillo! Vivo Sevillo!" muddling the feminine and the masculine; his knowledge of Spanish was shaky, and he was emotional to the point of tears.

The mother was carried to the palace where they were staying—the Palace of the Dukes of Alba—where a doctor attended to her.

The news of this birth to the fertile mother and the joyous ambassador was proclaimed throughout the city. Women from all the good families brought gifts for the ambassador's wife and her daughter, and some even called on them at the palace, ignoring the postpartum quarantine. The first few days of Claudia's life were one running celebration. All the city's musicians serenaded them at the palace gates (especially Teresa, who had the voice of an angel). Men stopped by to join in this endless party with His Excellency the Russian Ambassador, who was celebrating the arrival of his "Sevillian daughter" with vodka. It was said that, twenty hours after she gave birth, the ambassadress tried to dance a Sevillana—"tried," because she danced quite poorly, but she danced the whole thing from beginning to end. That's how Claudia came into the world: the sunny orchard, the fountain, and the lemon tree, all bathed in the light of the Sevillian sky.

Sergei was born in the Karenin Palace, in St. Petersburg, in splendid isolation, as if there were something shameful about arriving in this world. We don't know any of the details. It's a fact that both Anna's births were far from simple and painless. The second time, she developed a fever, she was on her deathbed (or so it's written), and if there was a silver lining, it was that her impending funeral brought together people who had stopped speaking to each other.

In her first birth—Sergei's—she didn't develop a fever, yet pain and anxiety dominated the whole experience. It's possible the delivery took place at midnight, that it wasn't snowing, raining, or windy. But the air was frigid. Neither grandmother was present; Anna's only company, apart from the doctor, was Marya Efimovna, an older woman who had just started working for Anna, hired to look after her newborn son. His mother's brother didn't appear in the palace for more than forty days, and there wasn't a single visitor from his father's side of the family.

3. Clementine Defends Herself

Demoralized by the botched detonation of her bomb, hugging her (considerably lighter) faux babe, Clementine walks along, observing what's happening in the streets. She notes the massive military preparations that have been undertaken without any fanfare whatsoever, with the utmost discretion.

She decides to stick with the original plan and return to Nevsky Prospekt. She calms down. "It's doesn't matter, it doesn't matter, there will be others. . . . Socialism and anarchy! The government is our enemy!" Clementine stops at the seamstresses' entrance to the sweatshop behind the clothing store on Nevsky Prospekt. The door is two steps down from street level. She reaches for the doorframe, feeling along the top ledge with her fingers for the picklock. She unlocks the door and returns the pick to its hiding place.

No sooner does she cross the threshold than she drops the bundle that was her pretend babe and kicks it, scattering the rags. Scraps of cloth fly. She picks up an oil lamp and lights it, then gathers the cloth scraps from the floor and rolls them up under one arm. She uncovers her head and neck, her thick mane is wild, and she shakes it out as she traverses the dark passageway to the back of the shop. Clementine puts the bundle of scraps on the table and wraps herself in her cloak once more as she says to herself, "It's cold."

Inside the workshop, which is large, no one sits ruining their eyesight at the sewing machines. Clementine once worked here, her family's breadwinner, supporting her grandmother and her siblings until first the old woman, then the little ones, died of the flu; her mother had died in another epidemic when she was five years old. She's a seamstress by training (one of the best in St. Petersburg) with the heart of an activist—she was relieved of her responsibilities for participating in a strike and briefly imprisoned thereafter, but since she's an attractive woman, they underestimated the role she had played in organizing her coworkers, ignoring their only informant, certain that he was laying the blame on her to protect the real culprit. That's Clementine: she's wary, and she's angry. Back in those days, all she wanted was for the wealthy to have some pity, to show some charity to the poor and treat the workers with respect, but that experience showed her how foolish she had been, and now she's a true radical. She exchanged her needle for a sword, and not just in a manner of speaking: she traded in her scissors and thread for homemade bombs.

The workshop is dark, except for her lamp and a timid candle burning in the far left corner. Clementine says aloud, "It's very cold. How can you sew, your fingers stiff from this cold? It's freezing!" She begins arranging her hair to cover it again. "Sitting here without natural light, in this damp air, how can you stand it?"

In the darkness, the deep, well-enunciated voice of an educated man answers her. "Eleven and a half hours a day."

"What are you doing here, Vladimir?" Clementine is taken aback. "Didn't you promise me not to use the pick again?"

"I had to. . . . Eleven and a half hours a day."

"Without stopping," Clementine replies as her expression fills with a different kind of light (her face is always full of light), one of joy. "An eleven-and-a-half-hour day."

"Compared to the fourteen they worked until a few years ago, it's nothing."

"In the cold, no windows, no toilet, no break for a breath of fresh air . . . with so little light that your eyesight goes? That's 'nothing'? No. Resignation is shameful. Don't give them ideas! There's only one solution: revolution! One solution: revolution! One solution . . . !"

"Eleven and a half hours is almost three hours less. Admit it."

"Revolution! They keep track of how many pieces they're finishing and always make them work more. Not for God, not for any master!"

"Their bodies may be freezing, but at least they have hot heads. . . ."

"Don't provoke me. The day before yesterday when I stopped by the workshop they were saying, 'Sunday we'll go to the demonstration. With Father Gapon,' 'We'll take pictures of the tsar and banners we'll sew ourselves, he's our father, he'll hear us.' Father Gapon this, Father Gapon that, their faith in him is blind, he's the Pied Piper of Hamelin. . . . When they embraced me farewell, I could hardly refrain from scratching their faces, they're so stupid. Over and over I told them, "The only church that shows the light is one that's on fire!"'"

"You came out with that old slogan? I can see their faces now!"

"And I told them, 'Better to die on your feet than to live on your knees.' And I told them . . ."

Clementine falls silent and looks nervous, worried again; she wraps her scarf around her head.

From the darkness behind the sole candle, the voice speaks again, now pleading, "No, Clementine! Don't cover your hair!"

He leaves the corner where he's been hiding and comes to her. He's very young, pale and thin, dressed impeccably. It's hard to determine his profession from his voice and his clothes. Is he a domestic servant, an employee of the palace or some other branch of government, and if he is, what's his rank? His coat is open; he trembles like an autumn leaf. His clothes are of good quality, but a careful eye would notice they're not made to measure, and the fabric's so fine they must be secondhand. His hands are delicate, not the hands of a man accustomed to chiseling stone. They tell the story of the work he's done since he was a child: watchmaking. His luminosity gives him an air of both fragility and fortitude.

Clementine uncovers her head and embraces him.

"Clementine, I went to Tsarskoye Selo to deliver a letter to the tsar on behalf of Father Gapon."

Clementine steps back.

"To Tsarskoye Selo? What on earth!"

"He refused the letter. And my two companions were arrested. They let me go just so the reverend would hear directly from one of his own that the tsar doesn't have the least interest in hearing what he has to say."

Silence. Clementine rubs her eyes and shakes her head impatiently.

"You should never have gone to Tsarskoye Selo to see the tsar. What madness! Why would you knowingly put your head in the lion's mouth? And they call the tyrant 'father'! They're done for! How on earth could you go? You're crazy! What a relief to know you're here, and safe."

"The tsar refused our letter."

"Yes, yes, I heard you, you don't need to explain. Vladimir, what did you expect? A message enjoining him to come to St. Petersburg tomorrow to hear the prayers of his 'children'? Another stupid Gaponist. . . . Never mind, you're here now."

Vladimir is ashamed of his naivety; the color of his complexion gives him away. Red as a strawberry, he changes the subject. "But why is no one here today? What's happened? Where are all the seamstresses? And the children who help make the lace? Are they going to shut down the workshop?"

"Police orders, Vladimir. They don't want laborers gathering in this part of town this weekend. They forced all the workshops near the Nevsky to shut down. So much the better for me: they might have taken me prisoner, identified me, come after my colleagues here in retaliation, and blamed them for something they had no involvement in. . . . And they would have found you here! I would never have forgiven myself. . . . I never thought you'd use that picklock again, we agreed. . . ."

"Forget the stupid picklock. Slow down, I'm not following you. Does this mean that . . . ?"

"Yes, Vladimir. Today was my mission. Propaganda of the deed!"

"Today?"

"You'll never imagine what happened: I planted a dud . . . a faulty bomb! It didn't explode! It hardly even made a noise, as if it didn't have any explosives in it. What a failure."

Clementine embraces him again, shaking.

"Calm down, Clementine. Look on the bright side: no one died. Calm down."

"I'm holding you because I want to. . . ."

Clementine recovers her composure.

"It's over now."

"Not completely. I failed, though it wasn't my fault. I left the bomb before we had planned to because they suspended the tram service. Boring details. . . . The fact is, the bomb was good for nothing. If only you had made it!"

"I don't make bombs, Clementine. I used to repair watches, which is quite different."

"But you know how to make explosives. If you had made it . . ."

She steps away from Vladimir again. She changes her attitude. She's completely revitalized. Handsome Clementine, a one-of-a-kind woman.

"Clementine . . . I don't make bombs. Understand?"

"Giorgi is coming to get me out of here at eight. Do you want to come with me? We'll take you to the Haven? Will you give Gapon the news?"

"I can't, Clementine. Father Gapon already knows everything, and he doesn't want the news to spread. That's why they ordered me to go into hiding until the demonstration is over tomorrow. I can't go to Narva and I can't go anywhere near other members of the assembly. . . . I may not have been afraid of delivering the message to the tsar, but I'm afraid of everyone else, Father Gapon's people most of all. I can't disobey them, it wouldn't make any difference. Besides . . . I don't want to go to tomorrow's 'prayer.' . . . See how they've given it a religious name?

I'll spend the night at my sister Aleksandra's, Mademoiselle Anya never notices.... That will put my sister at ease, I sent her a message that I was going to deliver Father Gapon's letter and that I was a little worried.... I'm sure she's worried too."

Clementine covers her head once more.

"Everything's turning out badly, very badly. Today they posted some notices . . . announcing that demonstrations are forbidden. Things are going very badly, very badly."

"The demonstration should be cancelled."

"I agree. No . . . although . . . if something happens, something horrible, a massacre . . . the people will rise up in rebellion, they'll forget about their prayers and call for the blood of the guilty. And that would be no good at all."

"Don't talk like that, Clementine."

"Some hero will offer to carry the red flag. It will serve as an excuse to kill who knows how many innocent people. They'll be the ones who ruin the prayer. Pointless prayers, but perhaps they'll suffice.... And if there's no red flag, what do I know, perhaps bullets won't fly...."

"I don't know."

"We can't fool ourselves. They've made it clear a thousand different ways. If my bomb had only exploded . . . they wouldn't have been able to continue with their plan, they would have called off the demonstration."

Clementine leaves without saying goodbye. Behind her, unraveling,

the small bundle that was, for a few hours, her fake child
a tangled mess of strips of cloth
another element of the darkness
becomes complete a few minutes later
Vladimir blows out the candle
and leaves.

4. To the Concert

At 7:35 on the dot, Claudia and Sergei get into their carriage. Just as the horses begin to move, Claudia speaks: "We're picking up Anya." Her words land like a grenade.

With his hands on his chin he asks, his voice strangled, "Anya? Why are you persecuting me?" Sergei can't bear seeing his little sister, least of all at the theater, where everyone in society gathers. He practically shouts at the driver, "Giorgi! Stop the horses!"

"Sergei, for God's sake, calm down!"

"You go! I'm not going. You've ruined the only good thing about this horrible day."

Giorgi slows their pace, listening to the argument—he's accustomed to them—but he doesn't bring the horses to a halt.

"We have plenty of time, don't worry," Claudia argues, trying to pacify him, because, to justify his reaction to going to the theater with his sister, Sergei has complained that he can't stand how long they always have to wait for her when they go to pick her up, an undeniable fact. "I took matters into my own hands, she'll be ready on time."

"There's never enough time for Anya, you know that. She'll take years to come down, she always forgets something...and..." Sergei wants to describe his revulsion to Claudia, but his tongue fails him.

"Enough, Sergei, she's your sister. This is why I didn't mention it earlier. To avoid a scene. We're picking her up, and that's final!"

Giorgi maintains their steady pace.

Time seems to slow down. Oblivious to what's happening on the avenue, Sergei sighs. "Farewell, concert!"

"Such drama! Don't grit your teeth, stop grinding them this second, you'll crack them!"

"I'm not grinding them."

"Of course you are, even when you speak. Stop it! Relax! We're on our way!"

"I'm not going to the concert."

"Enough. You're coming. You have to come," and she adds, in her high, confident voice, "Onward, Giorgi! Onward! To Mademoiselle Anya's!" The coach speeds up again, and Claudia picks up where she left off, without changing her tone of voice. "I've noticed how badly you're treating your teeth, as if they're responsible for these ridiculous fits you throw about Anya. Ridiculous! She's a sweetheart. Calm down, Sergei, it's all right. I asked her to be ready for us. I told her we'd stop by at 7:20 (so I lied a little). Everything's fine. I know you well, you wouldn't want to arrive too early. You're the only person in all St. Petersburg who goes to the concert for the music."

When the carriage stops, the door to the Karenin Palace opens like a jack-in-the-box, and out springs Anya. Sergei catches a glimpse of Kapitonich, the old hall porter, as the door closes.

"I heard you coming!" Anya says as she gets into the carriage, smiling. "I wanted to show my sister-in-law how grateful I am, I was waiting right by the front door with my muff and my hat on, ready to go. . . . I'm so easily distracted. Aleksandra was asking me to let her do the most absurd thing. . . . I refused, of course."

Anya's cheeks are burning, as if she's been sitting next to the fire. Sergei greets her with a curt nod, regarding her out of the corner of his eye.

Claudia asks, "Aleksandra, your lady's maid? The one whose patron is Princess Elizaveta Narishkina? The one who . . . ?"

Anya interrupts impatiently. "Yes, that Aleksandra, the one who worked for Narishkina, the tsarina's lady-in-waiting."

"What did Aleksandra ask you?"

"You know, Aleksandra is the girl who—"

"Yes, yes, I'm saying I know exactly who she is, don't you remember I recommended her to you when Marietta left?"

"Indeed! An inspired suggestion! She's a jewel, she's always pleasant and willing, unlike most servants these days, slow, two-faced, lazy. . . . She was asking for the evening off without any advance notice. Going out tonight, of all nights, imagine that, and returning tomorrow at dawn."

"You should have let her go, what difference does it make to you?" Sergei says.

"That's more easily said than done, Sergei! Who'll dress me if she's out? Impossible. Tomorrow is Sunday. I can't set foot outside the house without dressing properly, and without her I'm sunk. Plus, I can't do my own hair."

Without looking at her, Sergei mutters, "Who dresses you? You're a big girl! You can't dress yourself? And what's that expression, 'do my own hair'? 'Do' my own hair!"

Claudia changes the subject. "How was your day?"

"I saw two motorcars go by!"

"They're called automobiles," Sergei corrects her, tersely.

Claudia continues. "What did you do today?"

"I went to the Eliseev shop. . . ."

"Weren't you just there yesterday?" Sergei interjects. "You could stay home, you know."

"Tomorrow's Sunday! It's easy for you to say, I'm home all alone. . . ."

As if she's thinking aloud to herself, Claudia blurts out, "I don't even want to think about what your pantry looks like."

"Neither do I," Anya responds, speaking frankly. "I leave that to the help."

"You can't do *that*, Anya. They'll steal from you, things aren't like they used to be, you think you're living in your grandparents' time. . . ."

"I'm no good at organizing. That's what the help is for."

Anya and Claudia continue chatting for the remainder of the short distance to the theater; it's impossible to get a word in edgewise. Sergei stops listening. He goes back to thinking about the letter from the tsar and the impossibility of getting out of the predicament. He's so caught up that he doesn't realize he's missing his favorite thing about the concert, the delicious and childlike anticipation of what's to come.

The word "childlike," in reference to Sergei, is meaningful. He had been a happy child. He had a poet's soul, at least until *she* was gone, and to make things even more difficult, he was no longer an only child. His hair lost its curl, the color of his eyes changed, his gaze—which had been identical to his father's—acquired the restlessness of his mother's.

And something else happened too. Ever since he was little, his father had felt that he wasn't speaking to his son, but to a fictitious child, when he looked at him. Partly out of politeness, and even more out of fear, Sergei pretended to be that imaginary child. Then, when Anna died, Sergei became that child, the one he thought his father believed he was, a fictitious child. Slowly he became a man, and although he tried his best not to be a poet, perhaps something of the poet's nervous anxiety remained.

5. The Tsar's Letter

The letter that Sergei and Claudia Karenin receive from the tsar's desk that day announces the emperor's desire to possess the portrait of Anna Karenina by the "great master" Mikhailov, which, according to Karenin's will, belongs to Sergei.

Mikhailov painted it on commission at Vronsky's behest, when the lovers were living in Italy. The painter finished the canvas quickly (he was in a hurry to pay some household debts), but that didn't diminish its quality. It was magnificent, or so it was rumored, but no one apart from Tolstoy and a handful of others had had the opportunity to view it at leisure. And that was nearly three decades ago, because after Vronsky's death, Countess Vronskaya (Vronsky's mother) took the portrait down and had it stored facing the wall. And that's how it remained, facing a wall all this time, except on one occasion.

The note from the desk of the tsar ends by announcing his intention to acquire the portrait for the collection at the New Hermitage. Succinct, it's more an order than a request.

6. In the Theater

The Karenins' carriage stops in front of the Mariinsky Theater. The streetlamps illuminate the tiny, quivering snowflakes. Unlike the ones that had glittered in the morning sunlight, these acquire the dull, dusky colors of trampled snow as they fall, a muddy mess churned up by wheels, horses' hooves, sleigh runners, drops of kerosene and motor oil, and the tread of pedestrians. Claudia gets out, her eyes on the ground; the mess makes her heart sink. *We shouldn't have come,* she thinks, and her eyes cloud and glaze over, as if a film of dirty snow has covered them, too, as if she's seen the hangman pass by.

"It's January 8, 1905." Why is she saying the date aloud, is it to disguise her thoughts?

Anya repeats after her, "1905, 1905, I like 1905!"

Sergei looks up at the streetlamps. The light disperses the negative thoughts weighing him down. Anya scans the ground, looking for a place to step, realizing that she's going to ruin her shoes. "It looks as though a crowd has passed through," she says. "You'd think Pavlova was performing!"

Sergei replies sarcastically, "See the Broomstick perform? Not I, little sister!" The Karenin siblings don't rate the new star highly because of her technical imperfection and her sentimental interpretation. "She's an absurd beauty." "There's no soul in the way she dances."

A dark-green Mercedes limousine stops in front of the theater. It's Prince Orlov's, but the tsar likes to borrow it. A grouchy chauffeur sits at the wheel; a streetlamp shines on his face when the door is opened for the passenger.

In the lobby an old usher recognizes them immediately,

calling to Sergei by his name—and quoting a few things he said in the past—and to the women by their surname, taking their coats, hats, muffs, snow boots, and Sergei's cane. He doesn't give them a claim check in return. "Just ask for Fyodor, I'll bring you your things." When Prince Orlov sees them, he nods and immediately turns his back; the Karenins just keep walking. The third bell rings just as they pass through the door to their box.

The bright candelabras and the lively bustle in the audience restore Claudia's spirits. Anya takes the seat in the center of the front row, between the couple, which further irritates Sergei. They're in the fifth box on the dress circle—baignoire five. All eyes are on radiant Anya, her gorgeous curly hair, thick and dark; her elegance; her dense black eyelashes; her skin the color of old marble; her gray eyes set against the eye-catching shade of her dress, a reddish purple that's all the rage. She's the spitting image of her mother, though no one would have thought so when she was little. If she differs in any way, it's that in her features and movements you can see Tolstoy's inspiration for creating her—he once met Pushkin's oldest daughter, whose great-grandfather was an African, the Moor of St. Petersburg. When he notices people glancing at his sister, Sergei imagines what they're whispering. "Poor thing!" "And so pretty!" "She's exactly like her mother!" He's livid.

The fact that she's the spitting image of their mother is the main reason Sergei can't bear to be near Anya. He feels betrayed every time he sees her; when Anya's around, everyone thinks immediately of *the* Karenina and pegs them both as her children. But the truth is, though her presence magnifies the effect, it doesn't change the way people think. Whether he's with Anya or not, Sergei's a marked man because he's the son of that lovely woman who killed herself. Even the box they're sitting in is the very same one that his mother occupied in a famous passage of the novel that bears her name.

Sergei occupies the very same seat that his mother did when, accompanied by Princess Varvara (of the questionable reputation), she attended the theater in defiance of the way she had been ostracized for living with Vronsky. It was the very same concert where Madame Kartasova spat out "I'm ashamed to sit next to her." Today's letter has made him hypersensitive, and everything from the dirty snow outside the theater to the box that reminds him of Kartasova sharpens the pain of that insult, flagellating him, as if it had been directed at him. It's like a menacing cloud that burns and asphyxiates him.

But more than anything else, it's Anya that's upsetting him. Because she looks so much like Anna, it's like a megaphone is repeating, *You're Karenina's son; she fell in love with Vronsky and abandoned you. And what did she see in Vronsky? You saw something, his bald spot, you saw it from the window in your wet nurse Marietta's room.*

Anya had exacerbated his father's sadness, and even worse, she was a constant reminder that he and Anya had been written by Tolstoy. That's what he really can't bear.

What's wrong? Sergei? Claudia asks with a pointed look (because Anya is sitting between them). She also says, *Stop heaving such deep sighs, calm down!*

I don't know why my heart's so heavy, Sergei replies silently with an anxious look.

When the lights go down and the music starts, Sergei still feels the same; he can't enjoy what he's hearing. *I'm sunk,* he tells himself once more, *I'm utterly and completely sunk,* as if he's in his own personal opera, now sharp, now serious, now quick, now slow, *sunk, sunk!* It's as if Sergei's composing his own aria.

Anya is listening without hearing a thing. The music has a pleasant effect on her, apart from the fact that, paradoxically, it makes her both more sociable and more withdrawn. She deals with these contradictory impulses by picking up the mother-of-pearl opera glasses she inherited from her mother. The opera glasses and the relative stillness of the audience conspire to engross her in her own thoughts.

She moves the opera glasses in time with the orchestra, raising or lowering them in time with the strings, woodwinds, and percussion. Her predilection is for people who don't come from a novel, and of these, she prefers the least significant, the ones who focus their energy and concentration on experiencing every last detail. Anya's opera glasses linger on the tsar's doctor or his personal secretary, their wives, the hangers-on who hold unimportant government posts, the progeny of wealthy merchants, or the dilettantes who chase trends, or the visiting travelers. Over the years she's also learned to discern the ones who, like her brother, her mother, her father by blood, and her father by law, were born as characters, imagined by their authors, partly stolen from reality or flights of fancy as the pen flew across the page, but she's much more interested in the people born of a womb.

The opera glasses are an ideal tool; she feels closer without being close enough to hear what they're saying. Unlike her mother, she doesn't read anything but bodice rippers; she has no thirst for knowledge, no intellectual curiosity. But though she's frivolous and canny, she's not deaf, and she has a dark side that affords her a deep appreciation of certain composers.

When the orchestra begins its second piece, Claudia ceases following two or three different scores in her head, as is her habit. Wagner succeeds where her husband never does. Perhaps if she'd had a child, it would play the role Wagner does, but the child would have had to be troubled, because Wagner troubles her. He disrupts her natural calm, but instead of resisting, she gives herself over to the feeling entirely, teary and submissive as she never would be otherwise. She doesn't often cry, but with Wagner she has a hard time holding back her tears. If she had known they were going to play one of his pieces, perhaps she wouldn't have come to the concert, but she didn't look at the program, she was going to *the concert*. She was there to make Sergei happy (he adores music) and to keep Anya company, to get her out of the house. The arrival of the tsar's letter made the occasion even more appealing.

Claudia is not as beautiful as Anya and lacks that something special (or "exotic") that would make her a true beauty—something her sister-in-law has in spades—but she is hardly ugly; she has fair skin and thin, straight hair. Anya is lively, but her happiness is always tinged with bitterness, whereas Claudia is naturally happy, and she wears her happiness with beauty and grace.

Today, the difference in their temperaments diminishes under Wagner's influence, because Wagner is Anya's musical passion. For the duration of the piece, she removes the opera glasses from her eyes, and her excitement makes her even more beautiful, while Claudia seems distracted, far away.

It would be impossible to describe all the differences between the two women, because we would have to enumerate each and every one of their characteristics. But there's one difference that must be emphasized: Anya is a fictional character and Claudia isn't. Anya's cradle was made of ink, Claudia's had sheets from Seville. Still, it bears noting that Anya is different from other fictional characters because she barely appears in the novel in which she was born, and that gives her personality more breadth. Certain facts are incontrovertible: her mother never loved her the way she loved Sergei, her biological father hardly knew her, her adoptive one (her brother's father) felt tenderly toward her and wanted to protect her from the moment she was born—when she cried because the wet nurse didn't have enough milk, it was Karenin who got upset—but her very being also made him feel bitter, frustrated, and humiliated. These combinations of affection and hostility, tenderness and betrayal, and the fact that she's fictional (though only slightly so) make her a rarity: she's almost real.

7. What Giorgi, the Karenins' Coachman, Did

Giorgi, the coachman, heads toward Claudia and Sergei Karenin's palace. People call the building "Seryozha," which means "Little Sergei"; wagging tongues claim it was anonymously donated to Karenina's son, but that's a pack of lies, because it was bought with Claudia's dowry.

No sooner has the carriage come to a halt than a woman gets in, her face hidden by a veil.

"Thank you, Giorgi. Thanks."

"The master and his wife nearly didn't go."

"Why? They had another argument?"

"Same as ever."

"Are you sure you've got time to give me a ride?"

"Aleksandra, I'm not going to let you go alone. You have no idea what you're getting into. . . ."

"Giorgi, I know I asked you to do me a favor, but I don't want to create problems for you. And I do know what I'm doing."

"You asked me a very big favor. I'd do anything for you. Especially if you'll marry me."

"But Giorgi, you're already married!"

"Just a little. Not in St. Petersburg. . . ."

"You're married. Shush."

"Well, I have to go anyway, I have another mission. I'm giving someone else a ride."

They take the first eastbound street, and then turn northward. Two blocks farther on, Giorgi stops the carriage. He opens the door.

"Aleksandra, this is the other passenger going to the Haven.

Now we'll get going." He modifies his tone of voice, as if he were speaking to his employer. "Good evening, Clementine."

Clementine sits down opposite Aleksandra, as far from her as possible, and pays her no attention whatsoever. She's bundled in her cape and lost in her own thoughts. Aleksandra, by contrast, observes her with curiosity whenever the streetlights allow. Her clothing is most unusual; the cloak made of scraps is clearly secondhand. Clementine crosses her legs, and Aleksandra sees that under her dress, she's wearing tight long johns down to her ankles, like puttees.

The carriage heads southeast, toward the industrial part of St. Petersburg. It picks up speed, despite the narrowness of the streets, and leaves the city center behind.

Clementine is fully absorbed putting her thoughts in order. But when the carriage stops on a brightly lit corner, she notices Aleksandra scrutinizing her—Aleksandra's thinking the same thing she thought when Clementine got into the carriage, *Another one of Giorgi's lady friends, men really are good for nothing.*

"What are you looking at, young lady? What do you see? You like my cloak? I made it myself. And look at my dress."

Clementine unties the neck of her cloak and opens it slowly. In daylight, we'd be able to see that Clementine is wearing the dress Anna Karenina wore thirty years ago when she attended the concert where Madame Kartasova insulted her from the adjacent box, publicly humiliating her—the same insult that Sergei is reliving this very night.

The dress is one of many that Karenina's pseudo mother-in-law (Vronsky's mother), the Countess Vronskaya, donated to charity in a fit of wicked revenge, hoping women of the night would use them. When Clementine was let out of jail, they gave it to her because they'd "lost" the one she was wearing when she was admitted, a dress notable for its craftsmanship, in both its cut and its stitching, which some jerk took as a gift for his wife, daughter, or lover.

Karenina's dress is still magnificent, but not as much as it was decades earlier. Made in Paris especially for her, heavy velvet and light silk cut to her size and exact specifications, we won't worry about its original color, Tolstoy doesn't specify, and anyway, it would be impossible to recognize in its original state. All we know is that it was a light color. Something between cream and lilac, but most likely a pale burgundy faded over time, a dusty pink that stands out from the colors that are all the rage in St. Petersburg this season. The dress has a low neckline; it reveals the shoulders and hugs the waist with panels of silk that were, and still are, a paler tone. Clementine doesn't wear it like Anna, with a shawl that sets off her face, but with a sort of hat made from strips of hide that frame her face and cover her neck, throat, and shoulders.

Anna Karenina wore two bouquets of fresh pansies with colorful petals, one adorning the laces of her bodice and another in her curly hair, embellished with little feathers and a lace bow. Clementine has braided broken feathers together to look like flowers, tied them to her bodice, and woven them into her thick hair, beneath the hat, which, at first sight, looks like part of her cloak.

Aleksandra ponders this bizarre outfit but doesn't appreciate its worth. She smiles politely in silence, thinking, *Giorgi is crazy, what a strange woman he's managed to find....*

8. Intermission at the Concert

When the concert breaks for intermission, Claudia says loudly, "Wagner bewilders me!" and with a gesture that says, *I've had enough,* she moves on to another subject. The sensory overload has made her forget her worries. Her lovely white dress, made of silk overlaid with lace, still shows a trace of her discombobulation: the lace she wears to cover her décolletage is out of place, twisted to one side.

Sergei gets up, the last composition still in his head, Anton Rubinstein's Concerto no. 4 for Piano. He's moving toward the door of the box when a stranger accosts him. In French, he introduces himself as the new ambassador to St. Petersburg, mumbling an incomprehensible name and omitting the nation he represents.

"The person you need to meet is my wife, the daughter of Ambassador—"

"Yes, I know who she is, it would be a pleasure to meet her. But I'm more interested in you. You see . . ." He takes a step into the box, cornering Sergei. "I've read Tolstoy's novel so many times that you could even say I've memorized it. I'm overcome by the incredible opportunity to speak with one of its characters. . . ."

"Your excellency," Claudia interrupts, getting out of her seat; she's been listening, trying to distinguish a foreign accent in that perfect Parisian French. "It's a pleasure to meet you. Shall we go down to toast your arrival in St. Petersburg with a glass of champagne? We'll have plenty more opportunities to chat about a lot of things. But first we must welcome you."

Claudia offers him her arm, smiling, and continues speaking. "The pleasure is mine. I'm Claudine Karenina," she emphasizes the *a* at the end of her name, the way the French do. "Where were you stationed last? You know . . ."

She doesn't stop speaking and brings the foreigner along with her; he can't decline her company. Claudia is beguiling. It's clear from her familiar gestures and her tone of voice that she's cast the net of her charms over him.

Sergei overhears the ambassador saying, "When I read *Anna Karenina* . . ."

Anya has passed unnoticed by the eyes of this particular reader. Neither her beauty nor her likeness to the protagonist caught his attention. "Another one who forgot I was ever born," she says under her breath, resigned, and then, raising her voice and rising from her chair, "Sergei, since Claudia has been stolen from us," accentuating the second *a* in Claudia, "would you be so kind as to accompany me to the bar?"

She gives him her arm, and together they exit the balcony. Sergei is so upset by the ambassador's forwardness that he goes along. They haven't taken more than ten steps when a group of men breaks their circle, waylaying the Karenins.

"Count, what do you think?"

"About what?" Sergei has no idea what they're referring to. He thinks, *They must be going on about that stupid war in Japan again.*

A man with a red beard steps between them and begins ranting, "Anton Rubinstein, mentioning Anton Rubinstein when the Jewish conspiracy . . ." but no one pays him any attention. The redbeard continues, and the group does too.

"Opinion's divided, and we want to know yours. Is every Russian laborer a peasant, a bearer of the cross, a *krest'ianin*? Or have we developed what is referred to in Europe as 'the working class'?"

Observing Sergei's expression, which says, *What on earth are you talking about?* someone else adds, "It came up because of the strike. I think General Panteleev is right: we should raise their wages and sort out their housing and the problem of health care too."

Everyone has an opinion.

"And how are we going to pay for that? Our taxes?"

"The factory owners should cover the costs."

"That's a fantasy. The financial implications would put thousands out of work. The cure would be worse than the disease."

"Wouldn't it be better in the long-term to improve their working conditions?"

"That's a ridiculous argument."

"There must be a way to share wealth that helps laborers to acquire their own homes. And maintain law and order in the meantime. That would be some protection against unrest. We've had 550 strikes in the past two years."

"That's an exaggeration."

"No, that's the actual number."

"Zubatov had the magic formula: 'The only way for the state to keep the revolutionary forces in line is the cooperation of law enforcement and the working class.'"

The first man speaks again. "That's what I was referring to, Father Gapon and his followers."

"He's been called every name in the book, an imposter, a troublemaker, a Japanese agent, but maybe he's the spokesperson who could help us reach a truce."

"Or he's the chosen one, or he's got a personal vendetta. . . ."

Anya slips her arm out of Sergei's but doesn't stop smiling. Court intrigues and the vicissitudes of government bore her, but above all *these political topics.* Sergei has no interest, either, but it's a relief when Anya releases him, and he's about to ask another question when the young man who rings the bell to announce the end of intermission passes by, recognizing Sergei. "Count Karenin, a pleasure." His politesse and the twinkle in his eye chill Sergei to the bone. He thinks, *Is there anyone here who sees me not as a character, but as a person? Even I think of myself as a character, a character who's about to lose everything.*

It's no deep thought; it's the refrain he often repeats to himself, one Claudia knows well. It doesn't take a letter from the tsar to remind him of the bit about losing everything. He lost everything as a child. If he survived, it's because, without realizing it, he intuited what his mother said to herself: *I renounce everything I adore and care most for in this world, my son and my reputation. If I've sinned, I deserve neither happiness nor divorce, and I accept the shame, along with the pain and the separation.*

It's in this same spirit that he breaks away from the gentlemen's lively debate in search of Anya. He returns to the box with her, where Claudia is waiting for them.

"Things are going badly, Sergei," his wife says in his ear. "Lots of people left after Anton Rubinstein's piece because he's a Jew. How is that possible? What's wrong with people?"

But Sergei pays no attention to her. He doesn't hear her. He's bewildered, deep in his unhappiness. He nods as if she's said something banal. He just wants to enjoy the concert and forget about everything else. The music begins, and he lets go, completely submerged in the notes, so enraptured that you'd think he's in a trance.

9. Near the Port

Not far from the river, in southwest St. Petersburg, the Karenins' carriage stops in front of the Putilov factory warehouse, where the strike started. Clementine gets out without a word and disappears from sight in the blink of an eye. Giorgi, the coachman, gets down from his seat and goes over to a small group of strikers and activists gathered around a fire.

"Good evening, Volodin. I've got Vladimir's sister with me, she wants to know if there's any news about her brother. . . ."

"Quiet! Yes, I'll talk to her, I know who can fill her in," Volodin says. Without waiting for a reaction or reply from Giorgi, he walks over to the carriage and says to Aleksandra, "I'm Volodin. I'll take you to someone who will explain everything. Don't worry, your brother is fine."

"Has he returned?"

"No."

"How do you know he's fine if he hasn't come back?"

Giorgi leans into the window too. "I need to get going, the Karenins will be leaving the theater soon. Aleksandra, you're in good hands." And to Volodin: "Shall I come back for her?"

"We'll look after her. No need."

"All right, Aleksandra?"

"Thank you, Giorgi, thank you. I'm fine."

Aleksandra gets out of the carriage. Giorgi says goodbye and takes the reins; the horses set off at a trot.

"That's how children get run over!" Volodin says to Aleksandra. "They pass through the streets without heeding anything but their own desires. . . . They think they own this city."

They enter a dark alley. Aleksandra takes small, mincing steps—the elegant summer shoes she wears (a gift from her employer) keep her from making much progress through the snow, but Volodin is a fish in water.

10. More Specifics about Sergei

It's not easy to pin down dates in Sergei's life. In 1873, when
Tolstoy first wrote about him—Anna Karenina's son appears
early in the novel—and began to publish his story in the *Russian
Messenger*, Sergei was eight years old. An eight-year-old newborn. He's eight years old again when the first edition of the
complete novel is published in 1878, but a few pages later, when
the dramatic events of the novel take place, he's two years older.
So, for our purposes, he has three birthdates: 1873, when Tolstoy
created him; 1865, when he was born in the novel; and 1878,
when he appears in print for all posterity. For the monolingual
English reader, Sergei arrives on this earth in 1886, the year the
first English translation appeared; from his own point of view
he was born in '78 (though for our purposes, he was already ten
years old by then).

This bafflement of dates might help us understand Sergei's
frame of mind at the concert, a sort of trance that cannot be
attributed only to the arrival of today's letter at his home, or to
the presence of his sister, Anya, or to the fact that he's been
seated in the box made famous by Karenina, or to the comments of the ambassador recently arrived in St. Petersburg.
Because Sergei becomes so wrapped up in himself and the
music that it's like something out of a novel, you could even say
it's mystical, though that's not the case. When he comes out of
this spiritual trance, Sergei is resolved, an unusual state of mind
for him; he's not normally decisive.

His decisiveness is not the least bit voluntary; he's possessed
by a sense of resolve when he comes out of the trance the music
has put him in. He sees clearly what he's going to do. His life will

change. His features radiate an uncharacteristic certainty. *Today I define my future.* He feels proud, like a *real* man, like he's given birth to himself, jettisoning the inertia of his fictitious nature.

(He doesn't think it's unlikely, or impossible, that a being who's been given a fixed, immutable past can change his own destiny. The future doesn't fall on top of you like a gravestone. People create their own present, molding it, changing it from what has been in the past. But a being that has a fixed past, a written past, is by definition inert, indecisive, like a figure frozen in musical statues, the children's game. Someone else dictates the pose they adopt or lets them take a few steps. It's the music that gives Sergei the very real illusion of being human, the illusion that he can make decisions like anyone else. And he does; he seizes the illusion. He is happy.)

When the concert ends, the three Karenins leave their box. Claudia says hello to some friends, Anya receives numerous compliments—"She's always the loveliest," "You never look a day older"—and all the while Sergei stares at his own shoes, lifting his gaze only when Fyodor, the old usher, mutters something as he hands them their coats. Sergei acknowledges the comment, but he doesn't hear it, which is just as well. Fyodor's "I always remember your mother" would have been another blow to his spirit.

Back in the carriage, Sergei shifts his gaze from his shoes to the street outside. The two women are chattering away. Sergei doesn't hear them, caught up in his inner joy: *Today my life will change.* When they leave Anya at the Karenin Palace, Sergei shrugs his shoulders goodbye. The two women look at each other, stifling their laughter.

"What did I tell you, Anya? It's the music, see what it does to him, it's like he's on another planet."

Sergei doesn't hear this comment either, doesn't even notice their smiles of complicity.

The couple returns home in silence. Giorgi, the coachman, whistles a tune that the noise along the avenue prevents Claudia from hearing.

II. Kapitonich, Hall Porter at the Karenin Palace

Kapitonich opens the door for Anya. The old hall porter who appears in Tolstoy's novel is exactly the same as Tolstoy left him; time hasn't changed him one bit. Since Anna killed herself, he hasn't set foot outdoors, except once. He didn't even attend his own daughter's funeral five years ago; she had been a dancer with the Ballets Russes. He lives shut away in the Karenin Palace, dedicated to preserving it exactly as it appeared in the novel, with two differences: The first is that Count Karenin personally redecorated Anya's room when he took custody of her from Vronsky. The second is that the portrait of Anna Karenina in her youth was removed from the count's office, despite the fact that it depicted her before she fell in love with Vronsky and "changed." Nothing else has moved and everything is perfectly preserved, thanks to Kapitonich's endless care (and his fictitious nature).

But Kapitonich isn't himself today. Anya can tell from the moment he opens the door. His disposition, which makes him the ideal hall porter—the staunch defender of domestic stability—seems shaken. Kapitonich keeps his silence, as he usually does, but there's something different in his features and his posture.

"Good evening, Kapitonich. Is everything all right?"

It takes Kapitonich a moment to reply. Even more strangely, he doesn't reach out to take her coat. In a controlled voice, but with an angry huff, he says, "No, Mademoiselle Anya, everything's not all right."

Anya is startled by the way he pronounces these few words. "What's wrong?"

"Well . . ."

Kapitonich seems distracted, far away.

"What happened, Kapitonich? Don't keep me in suspense!"

The hall porter of the Karenin Palace looks at her as if he's just realized she's standing there. He quickly takes the coat she's holding out and, recovering his usual aplomb, says in a shaky voice, "Marietta went out!"

Anya understands who he's talking about, and she doesn't correct him by saying the name of her maid, Aleksandra, the young woman who replaced Marietta. She can't believe Aleksandra dared disobey her.

"What did Aleksandrina do?"

"She left."

"What do you mean she left? She took her things?"

"No, no, no, mademoiselle. She didn't take anything." The seasoned old hall porter is out of sorts, but he also feels the need to calm her down. He knows the whole point of his role in the household is to ensure its order and tranquility. From the moment anyone steps over the threshold, it's Kapitonich's job to make them feel at home.

"What are you saying, Kapitonich? I don't understand."

"Aleksandra didn't leave, she went out."

"At this hour?" Anya is still upset, she doesn't notice Kapitonich has returned to being himself.

Kapitonich breathes deeply. He won't tell her that Giorgi came by to pick her up and is her accomplice. That would be too much, he can't bring himself to say it. Instead, he says, "Three days ago Aleksandra received a letter. Today a telegram arrived. When you left for the concert, Aleksandra rushed up and down the stairs a few times. I couldn't tell what was going through her mind. . . . Then she called me and she said, 'Mr. Kapitonich, I'm going! I can't say no! If the mistress doesn't want me back, I understand, but I can't not go. . . .'" The hall porter loses his composure again. "She wasn't even going to cover her head, the poor thing! I insisted. . . ."

Anya considers her reply. She has mixed feelings; she's angry and upset.

"Did Aleksandra say she'd come back?"

"Yes, yes, mademoiselle, she'll be back by tomorrow morning, perhaps I shouldn't have worried you, but . . . she left some papers for you." Kapitonich puts them in Anya's hands. "Mademoiselle Anya . . . I tried to dissuade her. There was nothing else I could do. . . . She was wearing summer shoes, Mademoiselle Anya."

How could she go without permission? She's forcing Anya to dismiss her. It's upsetting because . . . no, she's not perfect, why exaggerate, but she needs her, and these days good maids are so hard to find. . . . With a distaste that threatens to mar her judgment, Anya looks at the papers Kapitonich handed her.

One of the pages has a few handwritten lines that Anya reads quickly, standing there, next to the door without her coat. Aleksandra writes (in clear handwriting), "My duty is to find my brother, who left St. Petersburg on the orders of Father Gapon to go to the tsar's palace to deliver a petition from the workers," a document that "you will find a copy of herewith." Since her brother hasn't returned, she fears for his life: "I must leave to find him: he's my only living sibling. I hope, Mademoiselle Anya, you will be able to understand. I pray that, in your boundless kindness, you'll forgive me. I know full well that you forbade me to go out. Please, I beg of you, understand that this is not a whim. I should have explained this all to you myself, but I didn't want to make you late, knowing that your sister-in-law wanted you to be ready on time." Etcetera, formalities that the poor girl took a moment to scribble, distraught at the possibility of losing a good job, because they're few and far between.

The other page is a copy of the letter that Father Gapon wrote to the tsar and sent to Tsarskoye Selo:

Sir: We, the workers and citizens of the city of St. Petersburg, from a variety of walks of life, our wives, our children, and our defenseless elderly parents, have come to you, sir, for justice and protection. . . . Don't refuse to help our community. . . . Free it from the intolerable oppression of officials. Destroy the wall between you and your citizens, and allow us to govern the country beside you.

As she reads, Anya argues with herself: Aleksandra's departure is absolutely unacceptable, it's understandable, she should dismiss her, she should forgive her. . . . *What on earth? What is going on?* She should have paid more attention to what they were saying in the hallway at the theater about Father Gapon. *What has my dear, sweet Aleksandra gotten herself into? And why did she ask me for permission if she was going to go anyway? How did I not notice how upset she was? Why didn't I give her a chance to tell me? I could have advised her, at least I'd have a better idea of what's going on.*

12. Claudia and Sergei at Table

On the table, elegantly laid out and decorated according to Claudia's taste, oysters await them and, for the main course, venison in almond sauce. The bread had only half risen, so the cook used it in a soup that's not bad but not fit for the masters of the household. Although Sergei feels exceptionally energetic when he sits down, the champagne they keep refilling his glass with puts him into a reverie again. He fantasizes about the future he can almost touch. Claudia tries to initiate conversation, but Sergei, absorbed as he is, elicits only monosyllabic responses, and few at that. When the servants come to clear the table, she switches to French so they don't understand.

"What are we going to do about the tsar's request, Sergei? Don't you want to discuss it?"

"I've already made up my mind."

Claudia looks into his eyes tenderly but with something like astonishment as well.

"And? I can't wait to hear!"

"I'll make a deal with him. I'll give him Mikhailov's portrait of my mother because I can't deny him, but I'll ask him to transfer us. Far from any city. They need men they can trust to work against the propagandists who are corrupting—"

"What are you talking about? Have you lost your mind? Absolutely not! Why would we sacrifice the life we lead? Sergei, Sergei, Sergei." Once again Claudia's eyes begin to search the dining room, observing every detail. She's put so much care into building the home they enjoy. She's not about to give it up for anything. And she'd never give up her Sergei either. "You really think you could be some kind of secret agent?"—here she lowers her voice, because in French it's the same word—"You really see yourself as a member of the Okhrana?"—she raises her voice again—"You wouldn't last two weeks!" She switches to Russian. "You don't have the backbone for that." Again she switches to French. "You, a member of the secret police! Impossible!"

Sergei shows no sign of being offended by her comments. He and the champagne foresaw it all. He begins to patiently explain, very quietly, in French, that if they remain in St. Petersburg, he can't comply with the request from the tsar's office, because he simply cannot. But if the tsar transfers him . . . he will gain favor for his unconditional offer to sacrifice himself, which is proof of his loyalty. They would leave everything behind, but in return, they would undoubtedly obtain the tsar's good graces. Maybe he'd even grant them some land (no serfs, though, despite the fact that the dream of his class lives on, and when he dreams, he dreams of serfs). Land. He doesn't elaborate on the detailed plan that he and the champagne have hatched. Instead he mentions something he thinks will matter to Claudia: he'll receive another medal.

"Moreover," he says, very quietly in Russian, "in the countryside, I won't just be known as Anna Karenina's son." He raises his voice once more and ends in French. "I'll have my own life. I'll be more than a character."

Sergei's eyes are shining. He beats his chest with both fists, exhaling with an "Aaaaahhhh!" and smiles. He puts both hands on the table and turns to gauge his wife's reaction. Claudia adopts a poker face. She speaks to him softly in French.

"You're not offering one sacrifice, Sergei, but two: yours and mine. It's you and me we're talking about. What will I do if I'm not living in this city, in this house? What will I do with my life, so far from our gilded life here?"

"You'll do something else. . . ." Sergei replies tersely, in Russian. Arising from the table with his glass in his hand, he walks toward the living room.

"That's impossible! Sergei . . . !"

Claudia follows him out, continuing to speak, waving her arms about wildly.

The idea of releasing the portrait of his mother for public viewing disgusts Sergei because of the scandal, the insult of her being exposed, and the rumors it will stir. Exhibiting the portrait will make life unbearable. Her suicide, her affair, the fallen woman will be the talk of the town all over again. And, once again, Sergei will be nothing but her son, the son of that poor woman, if you can call her that. . . .

"All that matters is the quality of the portrait, not the gossip surrounding it. This is the Hermitage we're talking about, Sergei! Be sensible!"

Claudia ignores the idea of a scandal; she wants to divert Sergei's attention and change the subject. "We must rise to the occasion as the situation requires. We'll say that we'll happily show the portrait to any expert they designate for valuation. That they should get a professional opinion. A specialist should come and evaluate it. We won't say a word about our instincts— don't think I misunderstand you—but this isn't about us, it's about Russia's artistic heritage. Is it a true work of art or not? That's what matters. And we don't know! We'll reply that it's a great honor that his majesty has asked about the portrait, but that the portrait is of sentimental value to us, nothing more. And that we're not qualified to judge whether it's worthy of becoming part of the collection in such an important museum."

"You mean they should send someone to do a valuation."

"Precisely. If it really is an important work of art, it will be its quality that matters, not the gossip. It won't be your mother on exhibit, but a work of art. Only works of art should hang in the Hermitage, because that museum is the pride of Russia."

"We'll tell them to come and see for themselves whether the portrait we own is no better than a Constantin Guys—that French painter who was just pilloried in the papers."

"Exactly, Sergei. That's what I'm saying."

This solution satisfies Sergei, but only for a moment. He refills his glass and his wife's. He lets the froth settle and says, "No, I don't think so. We'll have to leave town, that's the only way, we'll have to make that one of the conditions. Uncle Stiva always dreamed of Texas . . . of leaving Russia, crossing the ocean, living on the great prairie, where the horses are wild and the cattle roam free, the good Apache people. . . ."

(Who would ever have thought that this boy would get married, and that he'd marry well? Timid, indecisive—a pusillanimous pushover—beneficiary of a meager inheritance he had to share with his sister, whom his father adopted when Vronsky gave him custody after Anna killed herself, and whose paternal grandmother left her trinkets and kept the valuables for herself, holding on to every single penny both in revenge against the woman who was the downfall of her son and out of greed, because, as she said, "In the end, Karenin adopted her." As a child, Anya was the spitting image of Vronsky—so much so that Anna couldn't bear to look at her—but even this likeness to her own flesh and blood didn't temper the Countess Vronskaya's vengeance; so much for a grandmother's love. . . . Sergei's father's fortune dwindled toward the end of his life as his status in the government declined, partly because of ill management by an unscrupulous lawyer who took advantage of the fact that Karenin wished to stay out of the public eye and pulled the wool over his eyes. Aggrieved and diminished, he took refuge in the company of the Countess Lydia Ivanovna [an unbearable woman], his one and only emotional and religious support. But the old countess deserves some credit; she stood by him throughout the ordeal, unwavering. His Christianity isolated him even further, because after the assassination of Tsar Alexander II— who emancipated the serfs—his son, Alexander III, didn't look kindly on anyone who was not pure Orthodox. Old Karenin played all his cards wrong. . . . When his firstborn came of age, there was no one to look out for him. His uncle, Prince Stefan

Oblonski, had also fallen out of favor because of an administrative error that might have been overlooked were it not for the pressure Tolstoy was putting on the new tsar to pardon Alexander II's assassins and spare them the death penalty . . . which was just as impossible as salvaging Sergei's family name: who'd want to take it? Any woman who married him would take a name besmirched by that wealthy beauty who threw herself onto the tracks in a fit of rage and jealousy, in front of all the other travelers. There was no *apparent* reason for her suicide. Her jealousy was unfounded; the mere mention of a woman's name, or of some place where he might run into one, especially if it was the Princess Sorokina, made her wild. She convinced herself that Vronsky was about to abandon her, that his mother was urging him to make a more favorable match, so she took one step, and it was all over. She asked God's pardon at the last second, but not Sergei's—a huge mistake, because God has so very much whereas she was the only thing poor Sergei had.)

(Despite all this, Sergei Karenin got married early, to Claudia, a woman not without her charms, who was also young and rich. They've been married over fifteen years. They have no children. They get along well, their marriage is stable, their little battles make them inseparable. It's more than stable, it's an institution like the mountains or the ravines you sometimes find next to them; they're a perfect match.)

(It's easier to understand why little Anya doesn't even cross Anna's mind before she throws herself onto the tracks: the little girl never held a place in her heart. But her adored Sergei, whom she said she had given all the love she was capable of giving? She conceived her daughter and gave birth to her, but her second child was a stranger to her. It's not so hard to comprehend when we remember that she didn't want to have her; she was completely in love with Vronsky, and the pregnancy was unwanted, a biological accident. She herself said that she had already given everything she had to give her offspring to Sergei; the well had run dry. It wasn't that she was hard-hearted—she had saved the family of the drunk English gardener who, when he died, left them destitute; she took his orphaned daughter in and gave her lessons so she could read and write proper Russian. She provided for those helpless English people, but she didn't think about them, either, when she threw herself onto the tracks. She thought about Vronsky. Only Vronsky. She killed herself *to get back at* Vronsky. She followed through on the threat she had made hours earlier, but not just for revenge. She wanted to punish Vronsky, but she also wanted to run away, from herself more than anyone, as the author made perfectly clear. . . . Compared with Karenina's final step, her love affair with Vronsky is a brief, comic interlude, the intermission of a frivolous dramatist. The Countess Vronskaya wanted to tear her son away from the whirlwind—the tornado—that was Anna's suicide. She proudly accompanied him to the train station from whence he would depart for the war. She buried him with pride, and though he was no hero, she arranged for him to be decorated. "He gave his life to liberate our brothers from Ottoman oppression." Someone at the funeral had the nerve to say that if Vronsky hadn't died, the Russian volunteers would have taken Constantinople. For Anna, on the other hand, there was no mass, no headstone, no pardon. Vronsky was martyred for two causes: the Slavs and evil womankind. Anna had already sacrificed herself before she died—"A woman who can't be happy and prioritize her child's honor is heartless." It's quite possible Anna's soul still wanders the earth. Her soul doesn't deserve eternal rest, but how would we know? We're not mediums, we don't play Ouija, we're not concerned with the fate of ghosts but with those who walk the face of the earth, for better or worse, in the land of the living.)

(More about them later, but what about Vronsky, isn't there anything more to be said about him? He enlisted in the Serbian conflict, commanding an unattached platoon that he organized and financed himself—he was one of many Russians who sympathized with the Slavic cause and wanted to help their "Slavic [Orthodox] brothers" by freeing them from the "tyrannical oppression of the Turks." When Koznyshev [a faddish writer, the kind that come and go like most do, and a recent convert to the Serbian cause] went to the train station to find Vronsky before he set off on his trip to Serbia, he noticed that Vronsky's face had changed from a blank expression to one of pain [and not just because of the toothache that was tormenting him]. Vronsky hadn't spoken a word in the six weeks since Anna's death, had shut himself away and refused to see anyone, pondering his life—something he had never done—and flirting with death. "It's a sign you're starting a new life," Koznyshev said to Vronsky, more just to fill the silence than to cheer him up. It wasn't sincere; it was just a verbal pat on his shoulder, a gesture. Vronsky understood clearly that what he really wanted was to die, with dignity. That's why he was going to war. He was going to fight because he wanted to restore his honor out of vanity, and because he didn't want to live with the guilt. He wanted to prove he was a brave man, not the protagonist of some famous affair. He was killed by a bullet from a Krnk which was accidentally fired by a man from his own platoon just as Vronsky was bending over to pick up his hat, which had fallen off. A stupid, good-for-nothing bullet, which required the cooperation of its victim. . . . [The last thing Vronsky saw, clear as day, before he lost consciousness was the look of hate Anna had cast him years earlier, through her gauzy purple veil, in Countess Vrede's garden. That look of Anna's had been born for Vronsky; she never looked that way at anyone else, not before or after. . . .] But no one talks about that stray bullet. The version that became history was penned by a Russian journalist in the trenches, in lively language that disguised the inaccuracy of his facts: Vronsky, dressed in white astride his white horse, shaking his long hair and shouting, "Long live Serbia and Montenegro! Death to the Turks! Down with Mehemet and

Osman Nuri!" [the names of the Ottoman generals who were stationed on the frontier] as he charged toward the enemy army [composed of Arabs, Dervishes, Egyptians, and the well-trained Ottoman troops] and broke their ranks. . . . Approaching General Mehemet, he aimed his Krnk rifle and prepared to fire when one of the soldiers protecting the Turkish leader hit him with a shot between the eyes. And so, according to the story, Vronsky died, his thick hair [in fact he was going bald] uncovered, dressed in white [despite the fact that he was wearing an officer's uniform, which was a different color], a courageous man of action [although his toothache had weakened him significantly, and he was still suffering from Anna's death], aiming his Krnk [though in truth he was killed by his own men while reaching for his hat]. If the journalist's version had been true, Vronsky's expression would have changed the second the bullet hit him between the eyes, from pained to twisted, like a howl of laughter or a fit of delirium. But no such thing ever happened. . . . Every era has its own Vronskys, revising their own histories to be courageous and heroic, mediocre actors in their own destinies, obscuring the truth with smoke and mirrors, gilding their own stories, and making little difference.)

13. Aleksandra and Volodin Go to the Haven

Aleksandra and (her Ariadne) Volodin are walking down a narrow alley parallel to the wall of the warehouse, in front of which the strikers sit around their fire, facing a row of tumbledown shacks. The alley is unlit, but shafts of light escape from the dwellings at strange angles, which makes it even more difficult for Aleksandra to walk.

Passing through one of these shafts of light, Aleksandra realizes she has lost her scarf.

"Wait!"

"What?"

Aleksandra turns around and Volodin follows her. She hasn't gone more than five steps when, in a completely dark patch, she bumps into someone. Frightened, she utters an "eek!"

"What's wrong? Are you all right?" Volodin asks.

Out of the darkness, a woman's voice, one he didn't expect to hear, answers, "Volodin? It's Volodin!"

"And who are you?"

"It's me."

Volodin realizes it's Clementine.

"Clementine! What are you doing here?"

All three of them move into the patchy light.

"The same as you. This belongs to you, young lady, doesn't it? It's your shawl, you dropped it back there. Volodin, we came here together, in Giorgi's carriage."

The trio moves on in silence. The narrow alley leads to a storeroom at the back of the Putilov factory. They enter through a side door. Inside, dozens of workers are having a heated discussion.

"We can't put the women and children at the front of the demonstration. It's too risky. . . ."

"What's the risk?"

"The risk of death. You don't think that's risky?"

"They wouldn't dare shoot them. They'll shield the others."

"Well, look who's here! Volodin! With two women!"

"One is . . . I know you! Clementine! The anarchist! Didn't you say . . . what did you call us? You said you didn't want to have anything to do with us!"

"And I meant it. Not with you or with your Assembly of Russian Factory and Mill Workers of the City of St. Petersburg because you forget we women exist."

"Politics aren't for women."

"Not that again! Politics aren't, but work is, right?"

"Yes. Sewing, looking after children, things like that."

"But aren't we colleagues, equals?"

"We're different, thank God."

"So I'm supposed to just keep my mouth shut while inside me my heart's on fire?"

"That's enough, Clementine, enough of your stupid nonsense."

"We all have the right to change our opinions, and I hope that one day you will. Your eyes will open, and you'll see us as equals."

"Quiet. We have three hundred female members. Just ask Vera Karelina."

"We're an afterthought, the tail of the fox, not the feet, the head, the mouth, as if we didn't have the same rights as men. But I'm not here to argue with you, though there's no shortage of reasons to. I'm here to see Father Gapon, I need to give him a personal message."

"Are you going to march tomorrow?"

"Clementine! If you march, don't make any trouble. You had the nerve to call him an 'infiltrator,' don't you remember?"

"That was her? I sure remember!"

"Get out of here!"

"Down with the anarchists!"

"Anarchist!"

"Calm down, Father Gapon has been called much worse things than a government agent."

"I need to speak with him in person," Clementine repeats, unperturbed by this reception.

"About what? Why don't you tell us what it's about?"

"I'm not going to discuss it with you. Only with him. You won't listen to what I have to say because I'm a woman."

Aleksandra is listening but doesn't understand. She knows a lot about Father Gapon, but she has no idea what they're talking about. And what is this about Clementine being an "anarchist"? She's never heard that word. Is it the opposite of a socialist revolutionary? Or a democratic Marxist? A Menshevik? Or a Bolshevik? Her brother Vladimir throws these words around, and they've filled her head, like pilings for a bridge she doesn't know how to build.

"Stop arguing," Volodin interrupts. "They told me where Father Gapon is, let's go."

They head toward the river, to the flood-prone, low-lying land known as the Haven, where the laborers who man the mills, the furnaces, and the factories live in miserable, haphazard shanties without any public utilities. They cross the Haven, which could be a play area for children but instead is a trash heap where social outcasts live.

Thousands have gathered in the church of the Holy Mother of Pardon: men, women, children. Father Gapon is speaking animatedly at the podium.

"Will the police and the army dare to stop us?"

"They won't dare!" the congregation replies, voices raised.

"Comrades, is it better to die for our cause than to continue living as we have done to this day?"

"We'll give our lives!"

"Do you swear to die for our cause?"

"We swear!"

"If you swear, raise your hand."

Thousands of hands shoot into the air.

"Comrades, what if those who swear today lose heart and don't join us tomorrow?"

"We curse them! We curse them!"

Father Gapon begins to read the petition they'll deliver to the tsar at the Winter Palace tomorrow. He pauses after each sentence, and the congregation repeats after him—by now, they all know it by heart:

"We have come to see you, Father, seeking justice and protection."

The crowd repeats after him.

"We're living in misery, oppressed, crushed by the weight of our labors, insulted, treated like slaves, it's inhuman." Word for word, they repeat what the reverend says.

Now and then Father Gapon stops to ask the crowd, "Is this true, comrades?"

They agree with a roar, many of them crossing themselves, a sign that the words the reverend is saying are sacred.

Gapon begins to give instructions.

"Everyone should wear their Sunday best. Bring your women and your children. No one should carry a single weapon, not even knives. We'll have no red flags, not even red handkerchiefs. Come when you hear the church bells ring, bring crosses and icons and portraits of the tsar, ask to borrow them at your chapels and your workplaces.

He pauses. A murmur runs through the crowd. They knew about the clothing and the weapons and the red flags, but this bit about crosses, icons, and portraits of the tsar is something new. The murmurs are of assent; if the reverend has asked, they'll have to bring them.

"What if the tsar turns us away? Then we won't have a tsar!"

Rutenberg, the intimate of Father Gapon—the clergyman has thousands of followers but only one friend—joins him at the podium and speaks.

"We could be attacked. So I'm going to give you instructions now on where to get weapons to protect yourselves. . . ."

They boo, shouting, "No one should carry any weapons!"

"Apostasy!"

"Heresy!"

"No one should lift a finger against the tsar!"

One of Father Gapon's other lieutenants jumps onto the podium and says, "Is it possible to get closer to God with weapons? Is it possible to get closer to the tsar with hostility and suspicion?"

The congregation chants, "Apostasy!" their voices filling the church.

There are so many people crowded indoors that the candles flicker out from lack of oxygen.

Gapon begins speaking again, and Rutenberg, like a new convert, nods enthusiastically at his message of peace. Gapon calms the crowd down. Rutenberg steps off the podium. Gapon stresses the peaceful and spiritual nature of the march that will begin in a few hours. He says a prayer. He sings a religious song and gets the whole audience to join him. Then he asks, "Will any of you bear weapons tomorrow? Is anyone bearing weapons tonight?"

"No one! No one!" the crowd shouts in unison.

"Good. We'll approach the tsar without a single weapon."

Father Gapon steps off the podium, followed by his lieutenants. A young man takes his place and repeats Gapon's words to the people. "Comrades, will the police and the army dare stop us?"

"They won't dare!"

"Comrades, is it better to die for our cause than to continue living as we have been?"

"We'll give our lives!"

"Comrades, do you swear to die for our cause?"

"We swear!"

"Comrades, what if those who are swearing tonight lose heart and don't join us tomorrow?"

"We curse them! We curse them!"

"Comrades, what if the tsar turns us away?"

Volodin, Aleksandra, and Clementine struggle through the crowd toward the front, announcing that they have a message for Father Gapon they must deliver personally. They reach him as he's exiting the church through a side door.

Clementine goes directly to him, looking him in the eyes. She says, "This is only for your ears, I come straight from Vladimir." She whispers the password in his ear. Father Gapon takes her hand and steps away from his entourage to hear what she has to say. He makes a sign to his men to form a circle around them so he can hear in relative privacy what is meant only for his ears; in the blink of an eye, their backs surround them. Father Gapon leans over to hear her, and Clementine brings her mouth to the ear of this Ukrainian man of the cloth.

"The tsar won't receive you in St. Petersburg, Father Gapon. They've made it clear to Vladimir. He's the only one who returned, they took the other messengers prisoner and won't release them. Vladimir asked me to tell you that the tsar won't return tomorrow, he won't receive your petition."

Father Gapon straightens up and says loudly, "Young woman, I know all this."

"There's more, Father,"—now Clementine does not take care to lower her voice. "The center of the city has been wallpapered with notices announcing a new decree prohibiting demonstrations, on pain of death."

Father Gapon makes a gesture as if to say he already knows and it doesn't matter. Clementine replies, practically shouting, "Don't make the people march, Father. Your messenger says the tsar won't receive them and the police have warned that they will kill your people! You're leading them to the slaughter!"

Father Gapon stares daggers at Clementine and makes a show of blessing her with his hand before turning his back on her and joining his entourage while his lieutenants remark, "A crazy woman. Lord have mercy upon her!"

"No, she's not crazy. She's a corrupt government agent!"

They surround Aleksandra and push Clementine out of the reverend's circle. Volodin stays by Clementine's side, instinctively protecting her; he takes her arm and they move away.

As soon as the crowd is behind them, Clementine curses under her breath, "Damn bomb! If only it had exploded, if only . . ." Then she screams, "My bomb wasn't meant to kill anyone! But Father Gapon . . . he's not just playing with fire, he's leading them to the . . ."

And Volodin thinks, *Yes, Clementine has lost it, she's gone crazy on us, Father Gapon is the kindest man on earth.*

"I'll leave you here, Clementine. I have to go back for Vladimir's sister, I promised Giorgi I'd look after her. . . ."

14. Our Moment of Greatness

When his trusty messenger, Vladimir, left for Tsarskoye Selo with his message for the tsar, Father Gapon gathered his men around him.

"This is our moment of greatness. If there are casualties, don't have regrets. We're not marching into the fields of Manchuria, but if it comes to pass that blood is spilled in these streets, it will serve to prepare the ground for Russia's rebirth. If something happens to me, don't think ill of me. Let's show them that workers can not only organize but also give their lives for our cause."

These words cause a great stir, and some of his men become frightened for the first time, but they suppress their fear because Father Gapon often exaggerates. As if he hasn't spoken seriously enough, he adds, "Let's take a photograph before we say goodbye."

"Why say goodbye?" This last comment is the straw that breaks the camel's back. "Are our lives in danger?"

"No, no, no. Remember that I told you General Fullon has promised not to take a single prisoner. You're all safe. But as for me, my luck has run out, it's either prison or death."

In trying to allay their fears, he's opened Pandora's box. Now they know their peaceful march is going to be more turbulent than they had foreseen. Rutenberg, Father Gapon's friend, was the only one sensible enough to see that things might turn out badly.

This all happened a week ago.

15. With Father Gapon

After his encounter with "crazy" Clementine, Father Gapon greets Aleksandra with effusive enthusiasm.

"She's our Vladimir's sister," he pronounces as loudly as he's able—his voice is shot from speaking to dozens of crowds across St. Petersburg, in churches, warehouses, factories, the streets. He repeats, "Vladimir, Vladimir," so those closest to him will repeat the name. It's his way of asking them to welcome her, to reassure her that her brother will return from the mission he's undertaken for "the cause."

Father Gapon explains, "Vladimir was taken prisoner by the tsar's henchmen, those malignant tumors that feed off our father." He says this loud and clear despite the fact that he's received news to the contrary: that Vladimir has returned, that the tsar refused to receive his message, and that the police have taken his companions prisoner. Clementine's message was old news.

Father Gapon knows Aleksandra well, and not only because she's his messenger's sister. He knows she's a favorite of Elizaveta Narishkina, the tsarina's lady-in-waiting, a faithful member of the court and a Gaponist through and through, whom the reverend cultivates because she's his direct line to the tsarina. This is a well-kept secret known only to his inner circle; there's no need to make his alliance with Narishkina public. He's so careful about this connection that even now he doesn't want to pressure her to get the tsarina to intervene, to get the tsar to receive them. He doesn't want to test the relationship.

In addition, Aleksandra grew up in an orphanage where Gapon literally reigned for many years. Gapon had been the priest in charge of the Second Orphanage of the Moscow–Narva

Branch of the Society of Solicitude for Poor and Sick Children, the one people call the Blue Cross Orphanage, while also teaching at the Orphanage of Saint Olga. In return, he was awarded a church, which he quickly filled with followers, multitudes of the poor who went to listen to his moving sermons. Soon people who were interested in justice and political activists of all stripes started coming too. The way he celebrates the rites is approachable and moving, and his sermons whip people up into a frenzy. He lets his faithful sing their prayers to the tunes of popular songs and urges them to spend most of the service on their knees, which creates a feeling of belonging, of solidarity, of excitement, of fervor that's religious but social, too, and, according to his detractors, borders on fanaticism.

He's so magnetic that even nonbelievers attend his church, like the Social Democrat who was quickly converted to the cause, explaining that he'd never attended a religious service like Gapon's: "He's a true artist, he seems to see everything with his hypnotic, magnetic gaze, and to see through you, too, his face shining, his movements so gentle, so profound, his splendid baritone voice communicating a contagious enthusiasm. If he prays for the dead, we all weep, if he agitates for justice, we all thirst for justice, if he's celebrating a birth or a marriage, the congregation laughs and cries with joy; I do, too, even though I don't believe. When I see him, I can't take my eyes off him, I want to keep on listening to him even if he repeats things we've all learned by heart over and over again. He's a phenomenon, Gapon is a phenomenon."

Lastly, Aleksandra is best friends with Sasha Uzdaleva, the young woman Father Gapon took from the orphanage four years ago. He brought her to live with him when she was twelve years old. To this day, Sasha (now sixteen) is his companion, his concubine. He has recommended that she not see Aleksandra, afraid that, with her connection to Narishkina, word would get out about his private life in the tsarina's court.

"How could you have so much to talk about with Aleksandra, Sasha? She's such an uninteresting woman."

"Women's things. That's what she and I talk about."

But whenever Aleksandra has a day off—which isn't often, since Anya Karenina relies on her for everything—she visits Sasha, who, although closely watched, manages to find ways to escape. Gapon knows about every meeting his lover, Sasha, has (Gapon learned a lot when he worked for Sergei Zubatov, the former chief of the Okhrana).

Gapon also wants to keep an eye on Aleksandra, but from a distance, since someone might photograph them together, and if the Princess Elizaveta Narishkina suspected that Father Gapon was getting her Aleksandra mixed up with the members of the assembly, it would cause a commotion in circles whose reach would set off an avalanche he's not prepared to face.

16. Clementine, in Pursuit of the Night

Clementine leaves her brief meeting with Father Gapon wild with rage. Where should she go? She makes a spur-of-the-moment decision, and the minutes fly as she walks to the anarchists' lair. She hadn't planned on stopping by; she has no desire to see the agents of her failure. Which one is the imbecile who built the bomb that didn't destroy the tram and its rails? But after her encounter with Father Gapon, she desperately needs their company.

The group of her accomplices is small, nothing like the multitudes that follow Father Gapon: they reject all authority, they despise ceremony, they don't believe in any god or leader (Clementine included), and to all of this, there's an intense fanaticism and burning irreverence that borders on the obscene.

They call themselves Stenka Razin, in honor of the Cossack hero who led a group of bandits, insurgents, and fugitives—"Fear the wrath of my vengeance!"—who took on the tsar, the Persians, and the Kalmykian Tartars and was faithful only to the River Volga and his mother Russia.

It was a matter of some debate to find a name for the group, because they can never agree on anything. Someone proposed the name Samson Group, but Clementine objected: why would they name themselves after a man who'd had his eyes gouged out when he knocked down the pillars of the Philistines' temple, burying himself in the rubble?

"His 'I die with the Philistines!' is the act of a blind man."

She had proposed the name Three Hundred Foxes, after the ones Samson caught, tying them up by the tails and setting their tails alight before releasing them into his enemies' camps to burn them down. But there wasn't much support for the name Foxes. Stenka Razin seemed to please the majority, so that's what they're called.

In their meetings to plan their first act of violence, Clementine proposed putting a bomb next to the fortress where two legendary rebels were imprisoned, but they decided not to after thinking it over; it would be absurd, if not impossible.

"Who would even care? We need to do something that has an impact on citizens, not on prisoners, it's not worth the risk."

"What do we care about risks? Long live Nisan Farber!" Nisan Farber was an anarchist who stabbed a strike-breaking business owner and put a bomb in the police station, killing many, including himself.

Later, Clementine suggested planting a bomb at the statue of Tsar Peter on his horse, but they replied, "Absolutely not! We'll win only enemies doing that, it symbolizes the city!"

"But the city has nothing to do with that statue!"

"That's what you think, Clementine, because you live with your head in the clouds, but the people of St. Petersburg think of him as the symbol of our city."

When she thought about the city, what came to mind were the slums near the port, a ring of misery that surrounds it, where the working class lives.

"Then we should change the symbol to something that represents the people of St. Petersburg." But she didn't convince anyone. Someone suggested a café, someone else a hotel, they couldn't agree. They couldn't even agree on whether it should be a suicide bomb, to guarantee its success.

"There's no other way, the mistake is . . ."

Clementine is the only one who believes it's not necessary to take innocent lives, that the important thing is to draw attention to their cause through provocation—just not with collaborators or infiltrators.

At last they come to an agreement about where they'll plant the bomb. If they blow up the rails across the frozen river, they'll grab the attention of most Petersburgians. It won't be a suicide bomb. Clementine will plant it. They did a lot of strategizing and planning but didn't take into account the possibility that the bomb might not work. . . .

Clementine arrives at her accomplices' heated meeting. As she enters, she hears, "She didn't pull the detonator, obviously."

She jumps to her own defense.

"Of course I pulled the detonator, if I hadn't the bomb wouldn't have made the pathetic noise that it did. I only heard it because I have such sharp ears. Believe me, it sounded like a spoon landing on the floor."

"You weren't the only one who heard it—"

"But no one could tell where the sound was coming from—"

"No one expected there to be a bomb on the tram—"

"There wasn't even an investigation—"

"Are you sure?" Clementine asks.

"Absolutely. I have it on authority from an excellent source."

"But it didn't explode—"

"It didn't explode!"

"I'm telling you it did—" Clementine defends herself again.

"No, Clementine, it didn't explode, it let one off!"

"Silent but not deadly!"

"A real stink-bomb, we made!"

The anarchists begin to laugh. Their pent-up nerves momentarily turn them into a clutch of madmen, not activists.

"I told you that sacrificing yourself to make sure the bomb detonates is the only way."

"Keep on dreaming!" Clementine says. "It wouldn't have made so much as a hole in my dress even if I'd been holding it when it exploded. The bomb was faulty. It was poorly made."

17. In the Karenin Palace Kitchen

In the Karenin Palace kitchen, all the staff has gathered, except Kapitonich. In their distress over Aleksandra's escape, they're all speaking at once, unable to hear each other. They speak over one another, their tones not of grief or jubilation but of worry. Because they're so upset, they say things that they normally never would. The conversation slowly begins to evolve.

"Say what you want, Madame Karenina was the salt of the earth. She died because of the opium drops she took to help her sleep. Poor thing, she had no relief from her torments. . . . Each night she took more."

"Opium kills."

"That wasn't what killed her, it was what she did to keep from having children. That's what did her in," the old cook says.

"What did she do to avoid getting pregnant?" It's not an innocent question. The young woman who asks (Valeria) doesn't want to have children if she can't be sure they won't be born into a life of misery. She breaks her back working in vain; she tries to save money but her efforts get her nowhere: the price of a tram ticket keeps going up, her husband's salary (good old Matyushenko, who's at sea on a submarine) doesn't arrive regularly, her mother is ill. . . .

"The only one who knows what on earth madame was doing to keep herself from having children is Kapitonich." That's the cook again.

"How on earth would Kapitonich know that? Impossible! It's not a man's business."

"They say he went out to get it for her because he's the only one she trusted," the cook says.

"But that's wrong, completely wrong! Because when she was living here, she didn't use those ointments."

"Ointments?" It's that young woman, Valeria, again, stopping the conversation because she's got a personal interest. Many times she's thought, as she's mopping the floors, *Madame* (as they called Anna Karenina) *probably tangled legs* (that's her husband's expression—"Come on, sweetheart, let's tangle legs" or "He's already tangling legs" with someone or other) *many times with Count Vronsky, not just once but a lot, yet she had only one child in three years. . . . And with Karenin she conceived just one boy in who knows how long. . . .* To her, it's obvious that madame didn't have more children because she didn't want them.

"She wasn't using anything, for God's sake, stop talking about these evil ointments! She was a lady!"

"Then why didn't she have more children?" Valeria asks.

"I don't know. But Kapitonich didn't work for her over there, he's always worked in this house."

"She was such a good woman."

"Yes, she was."

"What are we talking about?" the cook asks. "Aren't we all here because Aleksandra left? We have no idea what's happened to her. Let's hope she doesn't fall into the hands of the tsar's secret police. . . ."

"The Okhrana? That's ridiculous!" Valeria says, laughing aloud, both innocent and ignorant.

"It's not ridiculous when you think about what her brother Vladimir was up to. . . ."

Magically, when she speaks his name, Vladimir appears. He hasn't checked to see whether the kitchen is empty because he assumed no one would be awake at this hour. It's not the first time he's arrived in the middle of the night, opening the door to the street with his picklock.

Knowing he can't turn around and leave, he smiles and looks over this impromptu gathering, asking in a faux-shy, squeaky voice, "And Aleksandra?"

"She went to find you!" the cook says.

"Where? Where would she go to find me? I'm here!"

"Wherever Father Gapon is, where else?"

Vladimir has been killing time, pacing the freezing streets. He didn't want to stay in the workshop where Clementine was once employed because it was true what she'd said: if someone heard the failed explosion and recognized her and made the connection, they'd come looking for her.

His curiosity spurs him into motion. Carefully, he makes sure no one is following him; he walks up and down the street several times before leaving. He ambles aimlessly, until, a few blocks later, he heads toward the tram station where the rails cross the frozen Neva River. He sees it from a distance, marooned next to the jetty like a forgotten toy. He thinks, *Unscathed! It's unscathed!*

He approaches the station. There's another man ahead of him, so lost in his own thoughts that he doesn't realize the station is closed until he reaches the ticket window. "Damn it!" he says, "They've closed already! There's no one here!"

He turns abruptly to leave and almost bumps into Vladimir, who is pretending to walk distractedly too.

"What's happened?"

"The tram's not running anymore."

"Already?" Vladimir says innocently. "Maybe the conductor fell asleep."

Vladimir takes the man by the arm, and they walk along the jetty to the tram door. They inspect the tram's interior. It's empty, and all in one piece. Vladimir scrutinizes it, looking it over thoroughly. There's not even a trace. He thinks, *The bomb didn't go off! Nisan Farber had the right idea, that's why Nisan Farber blew himself up. . . .* This thought burns in his mind. *My Clementine. . . .*

"I'll have to cross the bridge on foot," his temporary companion says. "Shall we go together?"

"Good luck! I'll wait."

Vladimir waves goodbye and heads off in the opposite direction. He's still not ready to go to the Karenin Palace to ask his sister to take him in for the night. He can't go anywhere near a Gaponist enclave. On Nevsky Prospekt, he joins the Saturday meeting of a communist cell whose motto is "Brave as madmen, we'll take heaven by storm." Protected by the son of a former minister of Tsar Alexander—the Liberator, who freed the serfs—the cell was where he first met Clementine, back when she was still at the workshop, when she agreed to organize the seamstresses to fight for their rights, before she was taken prisoner.

The last time Clementine attended a meeting of the Take Heaven by Storm cell, she bid them goodbye, saying, "If you really want to seize heaven, you must have a strategy or they'll strike back. We must seize heaven with our hands. To heaven with our hands!" The gathering listened, thinking she was crazy; Vladimir, on the other hand, fell for her. Or into her hands. . . .

Vladimir shows up and is received without any fanfare, as if he's still a regular. He sits down to listen. They're arguing about whether they should join tomorrow's march with Father Gapon—some say no, others say yes, including a woman named Alexandra Kollontai. She talks in such a moving way that he wants to speak his own mind, but they won't let him get a word in, he's lost his place here, he has no right to speak or vote, and they won't let Kollontai's right-hand man speak either; Kollontai herself has now left to attend another meeting. Vladimir watches the voting; the ones who don't want to seize heaven with their hands will march with the Gaponists tomorrow *not to seize heaven* Vladimir thinks, *but to beg.* He realizes his Clementine is speaking through his conscience.

After watching them vote and agree on a meeting point, he wanders through the streets awhile longer before going to the Karenin Palace, where we've just seen him arrive.

18. We'll Give Our Lives!

Father Gapon, surrounded by a halo of followers, gives his last speech for the day. In a hoarse voice, he repeats, "I'm a priest only inside the church. Here, I'm a man like any other."

His entourage has heard him make his pitch a thousand times, but in his exaltation, he can't stop, and his faithful followers don't want him to.

Aleksandra is one step behind him. She's fretting. She doesn't know a thing about Vladimir; they tell her not to worry, but without any specifics. She regrets leaving the Karenin Palace without permission. *What for?* she asks herself. *If I'm not even able to search for my brother....* She's afraid of losing her job, but most of all, she wants to know what has happened to him.

"I must go find Vladimir," she says insistently.

But they keep telling her the same thing: Vladimir is fine, she doesn't need to worry.

"Will I see him where we're going?"

"Probably not, but anything's possible. Calm down, it's all right."

They come to a place where beggars have built run-down shacks and bonfires; most of them live outdoors. Aleksandra has been put at the front of the group, surrounded by the men who escort Gapon wherever he goes, his lieutenants. Father Gapon repeats the same speech he's been making all day long, "We have come to see you, Father, seeking justice and protection." The crowd repeats what he says: "We've fallen into poverty, we're oppressed, we're crushed by an unbearable burden of work, we're insulted, we're treated like slaves, it's inhuman.... Isn't it true, comrades?"

Father Gapon's only friend, Rutenberg, steps up to the podium again, mentions weapons, and everyone suddenly becomes a pacifist. It's identical to his previous speech.

"Will anyone bear arms tomorrow? Is anyone bearing arms tonight?"

"Nobody! No one!" the crowd shouts in unison.

Aleksandra goes along, feeling the crowd's contagious fervor, she's caught it, too, she's possessed like everyone else. Without even realizing she's doing it, she begins shouting in unison with the feverish crowd, "We'll give our lives!" "We swear!" "We curse them! We curse them!"

19. The Karenins Take Dinner

The Karenins continue their discussion into the wee hours. It has nothing to do with the extraordinary quality of an oil painting that is exceedingly lifelike in its depiction of one human being. The canvas is brave and compelling in its expression of the conflicts and contradictions of an individual, uniting them all in one image. There are a number of reasons why it's such a pleasure to look at, as was its model. It has the gift of beauty, just like Anna. But Anna's beauty provoked a desire to possess it; it was irresistible to anyone susceptible to its charms. Although the canvas is scrupulously faithful to its model, that's not why it's so mesmerizing. Delicate, it invites contemplation of the color, the fabric, the craftsmanship of a hypothetical creature, capturing her beauty without her sensual magnetism, making the viewer introspective. It's a classic. Its creator, Mikhailov, had no idea what he would achieve when he painted it. He exceeded his ambitions, and how. He knew he had done a good job, and he was well paid in return. That's all—but *all* is nothing compared to this vertiginously beautiful painting.

During their conversation, Sergei lays out all the reasons why he can't stand to have the portrait of his mother on view for all and sundry to see. Claudia argues otherwise. At some point during the night, Sergei says it would be acceptable if the picture were exhibited as *Portrait of a Woman,* without disclosing the identity of the model. Claudia argues that it will cause a scandal no matter what. "People will gossip one way or another. They're idle and lazy, they don't have anything better to do. They neglect their children, loll about in messy rooms, and keep themselves busy with slanderous rumors."

On the other hand, they could sell the portrait and buy something big. . . . "A boat? Or a motorcar like Prince Orlov's?" She's trying to distract him. "Land in Texas? An Italian villa?"

The painting could fetch a price that would make many a dream possible. Then they would gain the tsar's good graces by allowing the portrait to be part of the exhibition, and in noticing them, he might grant Sergei the government post he's been wanting for some time. And from that post, many decorations would follow. The painting would help Sergei's career, not hinder it.

All Claudia's arguments eventually disarm Sergei, and in his exhaustion, he gives in. Claudia decides that she'll send a letter in the morning thanking the tsar for the invitation to include the piece in the imperial collection and requesting that an expert appraise it to be sure it has sufficient artistic merit for the honor of being exhibited in such a museum. If it's not a masterpiece, the canvas doesn't deserve to become part of the imperial collection.

PART TWO

BLOODY SUNDAY

Sunday, January 9, 1905

20. Anya Karenina without Aleksandra

At Anya's house, Sunday gets off to a chaotic start. Aleksandra's absence disrupts life at the Karenin Palace. Anya's room becomes the scene of a great quest: no one can find the bow for her skirt, the right color hat, or the petticoat that matches, or the collar, the blouse, the dress. They change Anya's outfit four times, without being able to complete one of them. The clock is ticking, servants come and go, yet Anya remains undressed. In the kitchen, breakfast still isn't ready. It's Sunday, but no one can go out to pray. Kapitonich is the most out of sorts; he doesn't know when he should go and wait by the door, and his knees hurt from standing so long without taking a rest in his room.

Aleksandra appears to be extremely disorganized, but chaos is her element, and in it, she's like a fish in water, finding things effortlessly while anyone else drowns in her turbulent wake. Those who go looking will find no trace of things: a pair of shoes hides a shawl, a corset hides a comb, a skirt hides a pair of knickers, and a belt hides a bottle of ink for writing calling cards. And no one has even attempted to do Anya's hair yet; that's Aleksandra's forte.

21. The Karenins' Reply to the Tsar

That Sunday, January 9, Claudia answers the tsar early, immediately after breakfast, in a style that is anything but bold and direct. Her letter says that nothing would make them happier than to see the portrait of Anna Karenina in the imperial collection, "an inconceivable privilege." They feel that, out of duty, they must ask an expert's opinion of the portrait, since they themselves are incapable of judging whether it has any artistic value, and the Hermitage "is without a doubt the best collection of paintings in the world" (it was a good collection, but this phrase was pure flattery). The canvas is at the disposal of anyone capable of judging whether it deserves this honor; let them come and see it.

The note is elegantly written (it doesn't mention money, for that you have to read between the lines), and Sergei almost likes it: it's so dignified, and it gives the tsar an option to decline. It may be that the portrait is poor quality, truly unworthy, without any artistic or financial value, a mere topic of gossip, in which case it wouldn't be worth removing from storage. With any luck, Sergei thinks, it will remain facing the wall where Claudia says it lives like a punished child.

Both husband and wife sign the letter. Beneath her signature, off to one side, Claudia adds a little note in looser script, "Not a day passed that my dear papa didn't remember the emperor fondly, always with tremendous respect and admiration," and she signs the initials of her maiden name, imitating the signature of her father, the ambassador. More fawning—or diplomacy.

Disregarding what day of the week it is—she fears that Sergei will change his mind again—Claudia gives instructions to one of the footmen (Piotr): he should deliver the reply immediately to the offices of the tsar, to the attention of "the Tsar's Desk," the subject "Portrait of Anna Karenina, painted by Mikhailov" That way, Sergei's anxiety will ease.

22. Piotr

The Karenins' footman, Piotr, is dressed in his Sunday best to attend the divine liturgy. *I'll take advantage of this errand to go to the cathedral,* to go and chew the fat with his friends, the only opportunity he has all week, since his mistress keeps him so busy all the time that he spends his life running from one thing to the next. He wants to deliver the letter as soon as possible, to get rid of it and go to the church carefree. So he begins to run, without paying much attention to anything. First he'll go to the tsar's office—he likes the idea of delivering it to *the* Winter Palace—then to Sergei's undersecretary.

Piotr likes to sing. Despite the fact that he doesn't have a single drop of vodka in his veins (he usually doesn't, Claudia keeps a careful eye on him), he begins to sing at the top of his lungs as he's running, a song he made up, or so he thinks, using a popular tune, changing the words as he goes:

> I bear a message for the Winter
> a message, a message.
> I bear a message for the Winter
> a message, a message.

Suddenly a chorus of voices joins in, mostly children, and his improvised song becomes a refrain—usually he would change the words as he goes along.

> I bear a message for the Winter
> a message, a message!

Although they've cramped his style, Piotr sings joyfully; being joined by this choir is heavenly. Since the tune is repetitive, his mind begins to wander, thinking about what he's seeing, and as he continues singing, he asks himself, *Why are all these people in the streets? Because it's Sunday? But there are too many of them.* He sings and sings, weaving his way through the crowd as quickly as he can, though progress is slow. He leaves his choir behind. Soon he's alone, and something tells him to stop singing. He looks up: the tsar's Cossacks are just steps away, in military formation. He says aloud, "What is this? Am I drunk?"

The ones who have vodka (and a lot of it) in their veins are the soldiers who are guarding the Palace gates. They received a triple ration before they were sent into the street.

Why are they here? Piotr asks himself in silence. He's in such high spirits he can't take them seriously. *Poor soldiers, they're freezing!* He gesticulates like a child pretending to be a baby chick. *Brrr! Brrr!*

He continues to approach. The head of the platoon, who's always on guard at the palace door, recognizes him. He shouts, "Piotr! Back! Today we're not receiving mail!"

"Back?"

He doesn't want to go back. That means he won't be able to go to the cathedral—no gossip, no prayers. *Aren't they going to let me through?* he wonders.

"What do you mean? I'm coming from the Karenin Palace!" Which isn't exactly true, because he's coming from Sergei and Claudia's house. But "Karenin Palace" sounds better when you're standing in front of the Winter Palace. *This doesn't bode well. . . . Or maybe it could,* he thinks. *I'll stay here until they take the letter, that way I don't have to go back, and if I don't go back, they won't send me out into the street again to run who knows how many more errands.*

"Back! Go back, Piotr! Go back!"

The order is so emphatic in tone that Piotr thinks—now he's thinking sensibly—*Why didn't it occur to me? I'll deliver the letter to one of the tsar's other offices, it's not as though I have to go to the ends of the earth.* Piotr turns around and walks off in the opposite direction, he knows exactly who to give the letter to on a day like today, this is a matter for the office of special cases, it's Sunday, after all. *I'll get the doorman to stamp it, then I'll go see that old bore Priteshko, and I'll have the rest of the day off.* For just a fraction of a second, Piotr thinks he might not have time to get to mass, where his friends are, but he'll find them somehow. . . . It doesn't cross his mind that Claudia is waiting for him.

23. The Three Women

There are three Alexandras in our story. One of their names is spelled slightly differently: Aleksandra, Alexandra, and Alexandra. Aleksandra is the disorganized one, with the gorgeous hair, which is unusually messy today, because she hasn't dressed in her own room. Then there's Alexandra, or Sasha, Aleksandra's friend, who's Father Gapon's lover, her hair so tightly knotted at the nape of her neck it's impossible to tell if it's thick or thin, or how long it is. And there's Alexandra Kollontai, with her short, fluffy locks. All three Alexandras are dressed with strict propriety, their high-necked dresses covering their décolletage. But the quality of their dresses varies wildly; all they have in common is their style.

Alexandra Kollontai is thirty-three years old, the same as Christ. The other Alexandra with an *x*, pretty Sasha (the reverend's live-in lover), and Aleksandra (Anya Karenina's maid) are both sixteen. But even though they're the same age, they don't look like it. The reverend took Sasha from the orphanage when she was twelve; she became a woman in the company of Gapon, who is a force of nature. She's matured from her neck to her knees, but the rest of her is still twelve.

A handful of protesters calls Kollontai "the Marxist revolutionary." Another calls Aleksandra (who works for Karenina) "the sister of Vladimir, Father Gapon's messenger." No one calls Sasha anything, except Gapon, who is too busy shaking his fist.

Kollontai (who spent all night persuading communists to join the demonstration because it will aid their cause) is marching with her group of Bolshevik laborers. Aleksandra is at the front, Gapon and his lieutenants behind her. As for Sasha, she's at home, completely unaware of this important event. She's not praying, like some say she is. Today she wants to stew some beets, but how do you cook beets? Her lover received them as a gift. She has no idea what to do with them and doesn't know whom to ask. She regards them with curiosity, trying to work out their secret.

So, of our three Alexandras, two are marching, and one is pondering a difficult subject. Kollontai says, "From now on things are going to be different." For Sasha, nothing will change after today, it'll be the same as ever, waiting for her lover (he gets home so late that she's already asleep, and it's not unusual for him to leave before she's opened her eyes). Waiting, and trying to understand things beyond her ken. She's not stupid, it's just that life is complicated, as they say.

For the other Aleksandra—Vladimir's sister—everything will change.

24. Claudia's Impatience

That Sunday, Claudia is thinking that they should get Mikhailov's portrait out of the attic as soon as possible, in case (though it's unlikely) the appraisers come soon. "It should be out on display, I don't want it to stay up there forever."

The problem is where to put it. Claudia doesn't have an office. The library is too full. The blue room, where it would look lovely, isn't a good idea, because Sergei likes to spend time there, and Claudia wants to put the portrait somewhere he won't see it.

But then, Sergei doesn't use his office very often. To be sure he won't see the portrait, they'll have to cover it. His undersecretary, Priteshko, who comes to the house three times a week—he spends the other days at the ministry—is the one who uses the office, and the portrait won't bother him in the least. Sergei can't stand Priteshko.

"I'm going to ask Priteshko to come every day so there's no chance Sergei will see it by accident."

Piotr, the messenger, is also carrying a note for Priteshko; Claudia wrote it in a rush this morning. It's one simple line, asking Priteshko to come to the house first thing on Monday. She'll tell him everything herself. All day—though in St. Petersburg's long winters it's more like all night—she'll wait for him in Sergei's office. After she speaks with him, she'll tell Sergei that Priteshko needs to work there for the next few weeks.

Piotr, the messenger, is also responsible for overseeing the pantry and the attic, according to Claudia's orders. The portrait is in a corner of the attic, but Piotr is nowhere to be found.

"Why isn't he back yet? I can just imagine, he's so scatter-brained sometimes."

Claudia is antsy.

Years ago, when Sergei and Claudia were newlyweds moving into their home, she asked for the things that had belonged to Sergei when he was a boy—his furniture, trunks, toys, pictures, and books. "I want our children to play with the toys you played with and to read what you read."

"Why, Claudine? I was an unhappy boy. My son"—Sergei could imagine fathering only one child—"should be a happy child, he shouldn't have anything of mine."

"You weren't unhappy, you became unhappy, which is different, but we won't talk about that." *Not talking about that* is the key to their marital harmony.

Claudia hasn't kept anything from her childhood—because of the life they led, moving from one city to the next, because of her parents, who were consumed by their own ambitions (which is how they were able to leave a modest inheritance to their children). That's why she was so keen to have all Sergei's things.

Sergei's childhood effects were all they took from the Karenin Palace. Claudia made sure these things—the furniture, pictures, and clothes—were stored in their new home, relegated to the attic. The three portraits of Anna Karenina leaning against the wall—Mikhailov's, the one Sergei's father commissioned before that (it hung in his study until she killed herself), and the one Vronsky, the dilettante, left unfinished. These three crazy women had lived in the attic for years; Claudia hasn't set foot in that part of the house since they moved in. "Fate didn't smile on us"—that's what she said when people asked her about children—so they didn't need any of these things. "What's the point?" she used to say. "Time is so fleeting."

• • •

At twelve noon Claudia decides not to wait any longer for Piotr, the singing footman. She brings two servants to the cave of treasures from Sergei's childhood—to the attic.

Next to Sergei's school desk—where he scratched little boats and hieroglyphics as a boy—Claudia sees a box covered in blue fabric and tied with a silk ribbon. "What's this? Isn't moving to a new house just like that? Things disappear, get lost, and eventually reappear." She blows on the box a few times to scatter the dust, then picks it up, taking care not to dirty her dress.

In the far corner, leaning against the wall, are the three portraits of Anna Karenina. The one Vronsky started to paint in Italy (a very poor attempt) is face-to-face with Mikhailov's painting (a masterpiece). The third one, by an unknown portraitist, of a young Anna, is next to them. Claudia directs the servants to carry Mikhailov's canvas to Sergei's office. The other two remain propped against the wall, in their corner.

Claudia hugs the blue box, forgetting that the dust will make a mess of her dress.

"I had forgotten all about this box. I wonder what's in it."

25. Unexpected Guests at the Karenin Palace

The time for taking a turn out of doors is long past, and Anya still hasn't left her room. Aleksandra's disorganization has taken over the entire palace. No one has any idea what time it is—it's after two-thirty in the afternoon, but everyone's on a different schedule; some of the servants are doing what they would at ten in the morning, others what they would at one in the afternoon— when a group of young men comes through the kitchen door carrying a body wrapped in a dark cloak.

The cook is snoozing in her chair, facing the door. She's one of those old people who nap all day long instead of sleeping a full night through. Although the young men try to come in without making a sound, it's too difficult to pass through the small door with an inert body. The cook wakes up.

"Aleksandra?" she asks them, as if it's perfectly normal for a group of shabbily dressed fugitives to walk into her kitchen. Seeing their faces and the body they're carrying, she fears the worst.

"We need hot water and bandages."

"A doctor would be better."

"No one will come. Bandages! Water!"

"What happened to Aleksandra? Answer me!" the cook insists.

"I saw them. The tsar's Cossacks came charging at us, their swords drawn, brandishing them left and right. Anyone who could, fled. People were dropping like flies, slashed to pieces by their blades, they were the only things standing between us and them. And still they kept on charging. . . ."

The young man begins to cry.

• • •

Someone will tell this story more calmly, of how the crowd marches toward the Winter Palace square in five contingents, approaching from different parts of the city and its outskirts. They proceed in silence, with a few exceptions (such as the ones who sang with Piotr). Children run up and down the flanks of the tightly packed processions, imitating the composure of the adults but unaffected by the solemnity of the occasion.

Father Gapon is at the head of the Neva contingent, the same one the young men who appeared at the kitchen of the Karenin Palace were in. His priest's cassock is covered by an overcoat because the warrant for his arrest has already been issued (this very morning the mayor invited him to the police station for a telephone conversation, but Gapon realized it was a trap and declined). He knows his hours are numbered, that they want to get rid of him. That's why he isn't marching at the front of the procession, with the bravest, most notorious and devoted leaders of the proletariat. That contingent is carrying an enormous crucifix and other religious icons, which they've just taken from a nearby chapel (others have had less luck obtaining religious items because the reverends have refused to lend them), and portraits of the tsars from the headquarters of the Neva Branch of the Assembly of Russian Factory and Mill Workers of the City of St. Petersburg.

Vasilev (the labor leader who is a member of the assembly) and Gapon's two most trusted bodyguards are also at the front of the procession, along with Aleksandra (the one who works for Anya Karenina), who is there so Gapon can keep an eye on her. In a state of nervous exhaustion from the events of the past few days, she's at breaking point. Aleksandra marches with the passion and contagious fervor she first experienced yesterday. Volodin walks beside Aleksandra, not because he merits a place at the front of the procession, but because he feels responsible for her; he gave his word to Giorgi.

All the city's dispossessed have joined in the demonstration, including activists and students, despite the fact that when one of them tried to say something, he was shouted down: "We don't need no students here!" In total there are more than two hundred thousand demonstrators. They broke their solemn silence only to pray in unison and sing the national anthem to the tsar (their beloved "father"). Obeying orders, they're all wearing their Sunday best—young people, old people, women, and of course the children we've already mentioned.

There's not a cloud in the sky. Ice gleams on the rooftops. The cupolas of churches and cathedrals are shining. The white snow reflects the sun. It all seems like a good omen, because it's been days since the heavens have been visible, and the temperature is mild for this time of year. But the omen is misleading, this is no day for ascendant stars. As Kollontai would write, "That day, the tsar killed something monumental in addition to the hundreds who died. He killed superstition. He killed the blind faith of the people, who had been certain that they would obtain justice by appealing to the tsar."

Although it beggars belief, official sources and reports allege that no more than three dozen people died that day. But for the Russian people, it was the last straw. The day goes down in history as Bloody Sunday. The petition they were bringing to the tsar, their letter, their prayer, goes undelivered.

26. What on Earth Was the Tsar Thinking?

If we go by his various biographies, it's impossible to know exactly what the tsar was doing when the masses attempted to approach the Winter Palace with their petition letter. Some say he was dining and even specify the menu, but those are lies like so many others.

We have it on good authority that he was keenly aware of the demonstration and that to calm his nerves he was bathing in the imperial bathroom.

The bubbles were a variety of colors. Beneath the foam, the monarch was squeezing his thighs with his hands, anxious despite the effect of the soap. Because at times like this, soap realizes it can fly when given half a chance. The heaviest bar of soap, the greasiest, the most difficult to dissolve, they all take off in situations like this.

Beneath the airborne soap bubbles, the tsar thinks. Not about the silent multitudes. Not about the prayers they sing from time to time. Not about the petition. Not about his childish delusion that he can fix everything. Thanks to the soap, he's not worrying about the war with the Japanese, despite the fact that it's a daily (and nightly) preoccupation. He's not thinking about his wife or his children or about the meal some say he was eating at this very moment. He thinks without thinking, as if the soap bubbles have entered his head through one of his ears and gotten stuck inside his skull, unable to find an exit, perhaps because they're too embarrassed to retrace their path, or because they don't know how to get to the other ear. His thoughts are like the elusive bubbles, fragile, empty; like the contents of the bubbles—pure air.

This is important because air is not a normal thing to think. If he had been thinking about something specific (even something trivial—*Why is that bubble bluer than the other?*) instead of being such an airhead, that thought would have helped him realize that he couldn't treat the crowd—composed as it was of children, women, laborers, the homeless, and others—like they were organized rebels. Because reliable sources confirm that the tsar gave orders to treat them like rebels. A soap bubble isn't a rebel, it's an uncontainable emptiness (though that goes without saying, we're just trying to shed a little light on the bathing tsar). Because rebels bear arms. Because the leaders of a rebellion are crushed by the powers that be. If the tsar hadn't been such an airhead, he would have done something to prevent the catastrophe that would lead to his downfall. Which was unthinkable to him, because how could anything bring about the downfall of the tsar himself? The tsar, elevated so far above all others. The tsar, who made a grave error in thinking that the people coming to him for mercy were rebels. They weren't. Oh, all right, a handful were rebels—Kollontai is a prime example—but the rest weren't.

The Imperial Guard receives the order to attack the crowd—though not from the tsar; he can't give orders because he's covered in a blanket of soap bubbles. His brother may have given the order, but others say it was his uncle, and yet others say no order was given, that the horses' panic spread from their hooves to the Cossacks' swords and the infantry's triggers.

And this panic manifested itself in drawn swords and bullets, or perhaps it *was* an order to attack—history favors the latter, but it's such a stupid mistake that common sense favors the former, even if it's not true—and some say the Cossacks came down the stairs in military formation, their polished boots treading each step in a dance of death. But there weren't any stairs. Let's not confuse the issue further.

The news doesn't spread quickly through the avenues, streets, canals, and rivers of the city, it meanders in a daze, and that's why most Petersburgians spend the next few hours as if it's any old Sunday, which would have been the case for Anya, too, if it weren't for Aleksandra.

27. Back in the Karenin Palace Kitchen

"What I heard was bullets, ma'am. Before the swords, there were bullets. We were two hundred feet from the Narva Triumphal Arch, we could see the river. The soldiers fired three times into the air. The fourth shot was the signal to charge. They kept firing until they were out of ammunition. Then the Cossacks came at us."

An older man who's sweating excessively is speaking. His hands are covered in blood, and he has a cut on his cheek that's barely bleeding, as if it's in shock too.

Whether it was bullets or steel, there's a body in front of them wrapped in a cloak, lying on the kitchen table. Blood begins to trickle across the surface, slow and thick. The cloak is the body's shroud. The dark, slow, lazy blood is its voice.

Young Valeria has already gone to tell lovely Anya, who comes right away, without stockings (she's still in the process of getting dressed), her bare feet inside boots that don't match the floor-length skirt she has to hold up with her hands because they can't find the belt.

"What happened? What's going on here?"

"The tsar's men shot at us."

"Where?" Anya asks.

"We were marching up to the Narva Arch."

"It was swords, not bullets!"

"It *was* bullets."

"They came at us with bullets and swords."

"Hundreds of people are dead."

"Volodin fell, I saw him dead, he's dead."

"Yes, hundreds died. And even more are wounded."

"And Aleksandra?" Anya asks.

None of the unexpected guests remembers what the workers were chanting: "Eight hours, Father"—that's what they call the tsar—"eight hours! We want an eight-hour workday!"

"Answer me! Where is Aleksandra?"

Loyal Kapitonich, the hall porter, rushes in after Mademoiselle Anya (he hates the kitchen, it's full of things that turn his stomach, especially animal parts, but beets too)—he heard her running down the staircase (the heels on the boots she's wearing are scandalous), and after looking in the drawing room and the dining room, he's come to look for her here.

Anya notices the body wrapped on the table. Carefully but decisively she lifts the cloak that covers the bloody form.

Lying there on the kitchen table, they recognize her.

"My Aleksandra? Aleksandra! Aleksandra!"

It's impossible for Aleksandra to hear Anya, because she is frozen in time, her attention focused on one never-ending moment: *The gray faces of the poorly dressed, underfed workers look dead, apart from their eyes, which burn with anger in this ill-fated uprising. Suddenly the battalion of Cossacks charges at us, their swords drawn. I saw them brandishing their swords. One blade slit Volodin's throat.*

The men who carried the body (not Father Gapon's hired guards, who turned and fled in the stampede without a thought for anyone but themselves, although some say they were martyred by the Cossacks), the ones who risked being trampled by the horses when the infantry moved out of the way, are speaking quietly, transformed by the horror.

Young Valeria is the one who says what everyone else is thinking.

"She's dying!"

The silence is heavy, like the blood that has begun to drip onto the floor. They peer at Aleksandra's pale face. For a second she opens her eyes, perhaps just a reflex.

"She's not breathing!"

"She's dead!"

Old Kapitonich ages years in an instant, all the years that have been waiting to catch up with him. Suddenly, all at once. No one there realizes it has happened. He still has enough strength to make the necessary arrangements under the circumstances. He goes to the front door and calls, in a decrepit, trembling voice, for Giorgi, who's two doors down, waiting for a lovely servant in a trance, and asks him to fetch a doctor. When he hears Kapitonich's voice and sees how he's standing, Giorgi thinks it's for Kapitonich himself.

"What's wrong, Kapitonich?"

"Hurry, Giorgi, Aleksandra is wounded, didn't you see those men come in?"

"I was over there, waiting for the beautiful Tatiana, I didn't see anyone. What happened?"

Kapitonich asks him to do two more things: deliver the news to the Karenins and find a shop that's open to buy the black cloth they'll need to hang on the front door. Giorgi bursts into tears when he asks for the black cloth, thinking about lovely Aleksandra, then he wipes his eyes and gets onto the carriage, guiding the horses between fits of tears as he howls, "Aleksandra, I delivered you to your death! Aleksandraaa!"

Kapitonich doesn't hear Giorgi's lament because he goes back inside the Karenin Palace to find Vladimir. He's in the servants' quarters, tinkering with a figure he made out of tiny pieces of wire for his sister. It's a little man who lifts his hat when you pull a string. Kapitonich delivers the news gently and sincerely enough to keep him from going into hysterics. The figure Vladimir holds in his hands keeps raising his hat as Vladimir sits there, paralyzed. He refuses to see his sister's body. After a few minutes, he begins to cry. Kapitonich takes the wire figure from his hands and leaves it on Aleksandra's nightstand. He has to leave Vladimir alone with his tears so he can open the door for the doctor, who has just arrived.

The doctor sees Kapitonich's face and is the first to realize how much he has aged. But he doesn't have a chance to ask him why, because Kapitonich guides him to the kitchen, shuffling along like an old man, and leaves him at the open doorway. No explanation is necessary. Aleksandra lies on the table, her blood dripping onto the floor.

At the same time, Piotr comes singing through the street door, but no one hears him.

Kapitonich returns to find Vladimir, but he's no longer there. He's slipped out of the Karenin Palace so he doesn't have to see Aleksandra. Kapitonich shuffles back to the kitchen, but his femur and hip don't cooperate, and the old man falls to the floor like a sack of potatoes. With the little voice he has left, he cries, "Help me! Help!" His arm is shattered, but no one hears his cries of pain because frightened Piotr is singing a funeral song at the top of his lungs.

"May her soul rest in peace."

The doctor completes the death certificate with the name, date, and cause of death Anya provides. Aleksandra will get a proper burial. He leaves without bidding them goodbye and is halfway home when Giorgi reaches him with the news that Kapitonich has had an accident. The doctor returns to treat him.

Valeria finds the little wire figure. "I don't know where it came from, but it will be perfect for my Matyushenko when he returns from the bottom of the sea." Pulling the string of the little doll, watching it lift its hat over and over again, Valeria says, "I hate that damn submarine. I hate that damn submarine." She puts the wire figure in her trunk.

Vladimir never returns to the Karenin Palace; he doesn't reply to Anya's requests to come and collect his sister's effects. Giorgi can't find him anywhere. "It's like Vladimir vanished into thin air."

28. The Reverend's Beard

Father Gapon is crushed. When his contingent of demonstrators is attacked and stampeded, he's saved by the bodies of the wounded and the dead—Volodin being one of these human shields. As he lies there, he says, "There is no tsar, there is no God." He repeats the phrase two more times, thinking of his Sasha, and says aloud, "Sasha, Sasha," but no one hears him because they're all repeating what he's just said: "There is no tsar, there is no God."

Rutenberg, his only friend, rescues him and takes him to one of the doorways in the square. There's no time to lose. Rutenberg has scissors and a blade in his pocket, he becomes an emergency barber, he shaves Gapon clean—farewell, beard; farewell, hair—and his followers scramble for the locks that are falling as if they're sacred relics. He changes him out of his long robes into the clothes of a regular laborer and takes him to hide in the home of Maxim Gorky, the writer. It's funny how the heart of Gapon's movement was made up of all the wretched people living in the Haven, a scene that resembled one out of Gorky's work, and now he's ended up seeking refuge from this very author. . . . But this crazy twist of fate is nothing in comparison to what awaits him, though that's none of our business for the time being.

PART THREE

KARENINA'S PORTRAIT

Three Months Later

29. Karenina's Portrait

Sergei has seen Mikhailov's portrait of Anna Karenina only once. The lighting wasn't ideal. Sergei was still a boy, despite everyone insisting he was already a man. He was on the way home from school. The Countess Vronskaya sent the portrait at the precise hour she thought Sergei would arrive. She had planned this carefully; it was her revenge against the son of the woman who had ruined her own.

The portrait was borne by one of the countess's servants—dressed impeccably in French livery—followed by two others, not quite so well dressed (although she was rich, the Countess Vronskaya counted every ruble, her servants lived with their bellies half-empty, and creditors had to call on her three or four times before she would part with a single kopeck). Rich but stingy, she squandered her wealth on frivolities. Such as? A feather from the farthest corner of the universe to replace the one on a hat she despised; Turkish delight from smugglers, which she shared with no one; fine Belgian lace miniatures she caressed with her fingertips before putting them away in drawers to keep them from being ruined; or French bonbons.

The footman in elegant French livery held the portrait of Anna Karenina by its gold-leaf frame, perhaps an excessive impulse of Vronsky's that, to a finer eye, didn't complement the delicate color of Anna's dress. Iridescent feathers for the mother, gaudy gold leaf for the son.

The second servant—in his thick felt shoes, his coarse clothes—carried a woman's dress in his arms, the only one of Anna's that the countess had kept (the rest, as previously mentioned, had been donated to a charity next to Olga's Poorhouse, which helped fallen women, because it pleased the countess to think about floozies wearing them). The third footman—his socks so threadbare it would set your teeth on edge—carried in his right hand the blue box in which Anna had stored her manuscript, and over his left shoulder, a huge, green cloth sack, which contained her collected correspondence and calling cards.

They also delivered a letter from the Countess Vronskaya, a curt, sloppy note to the widower Karenin, saying she would keep Anna Karenina's jewels for Anya, both the ones he had given her himself and the ones from her son. Karenin understood that these lies were intended only to wound him.

The arrival of the portrait and its entourage at the Karenin Palace had the effect the countess desired, but not in the way she had imagined. Sergei was on his way home. He was returning from school, his eyes glued to the ground. In the morning, walking in the opposite direction, he had almost stepped on a sparrow recently hatched from its shell, its bony body half covered in bluish down, still breathing. The sight frightened and disgusted him. This creature, grayish like a piece of the sky, its beak soft as cartilage, its feet disfigured, looked more like an insect or entrails than a bird. Sergei was afraid of seeing the sparrow again, terrified of stepping on it. That's why he was scouring the ground anxiously, searching but hoping not to find the little bird. His eyes darted from the ground to his waist and back, a somber zigzag. He looked up when he heard Kapitonich's voice say, "Heavens!"

It was the third time in a row that Kapitonich had uttered these two syllables. Sergei, absorbed in his search for the harmless creature, staring at the ground, submerging all his worries in this search, anxious but relieved of his other anxieties, didn't hear him.

He was about to be sent away to boarding school. He was afraid; he didn't want to go, but he had to, he knew there was no alternative; three nights ago he had wet the bed, which he had never done before, not even when he was really little. Inside him a storm raged, one he couldn't describe to anyone, not even himself.

And now, on top of that, the unflappable Kapitonich had uttered a worried "Heavens!" like another sparrow falling from its nest, half-formed. Sergei looked up. If it hadn't been for Kapitonich, the Countess Vronskaya's servants would have entered the house without Sergei setting eyes on them. But the countess's plans came to fruition, thanks to Kapitonich's unwitting aid. That's how Sergei came face-to-face with this perfect image of Anna Karenina, looking more like herself than she did in real life, her face uncovered, her lovely neck and shoulders partially bared by her Italian dress, her thick, curly, black hair, her eyes, her magnificent mouth expressing intelligence, honesty, passion, her skin like old marble, a color unknown in those climes.

The portrait, the woman, walked along without touching the ground; she didn't float through the air, because from her waist to the ground, she appeared to wear a pair of trousers belonging to the dark suit of the man who was carrying her. She looked like a huge woman with a short pair of man's legs. Immobile from the waist up, her legs took nervous steps. The servant was walking like that because of the awkwardness of carrying the portrait and his moral burden, aware of the countess's wicked intentions to hurt the boy.

Once upon a time, Sergei had played a game pretending to be one person with Marietta (his nanny). They used men's clothes: a shirt that buttoned from the waist to the neck and a pair of shoes. Sergei wore the shirt back to front, the opening at his back, but he didn't put his arms in the sleeves; he put his hands in the shoes and used them to lean on a chair.

Marietta hid behind Sergei and put her arms through the shirt. She'd move her arms and he'd move his "feet," talking and singing. It was hilarious because of the disproportions: Sergei looked like some kind of strange dwarf. Anna split her sides laughing—that's another thing Tolstoy forgot: Karenina loved to laugh.

The creature formed by the framed painting and its bearer appeared to parody the game Sergei played with Marietta, except that it didn't look like a dwarf: it was his mother from the waist up, larger than life, wearing a pair of tiny trousers. It was grotesque, causing Kapitonich to utter "heavens" and plunging Sergei into pain and horror.

The boy who was ashamed to miss his mother—who nursed the secret of his grief in private, who struggled with both the reality that she was dead and that death would come for him, too, especially if *she* came for him—was confronted by her in the light of day at the front door of his house. *She* appeared, her very self (apart from someone else's legs), the dead become death.

The footman who was carrying her slowed to a stop outside the Karenin Palace and put the portrait down on its side. Anna, floating above the street, as if she were lying down in the boy's bed to help him go to sleep after reading him a bedtime story. Anna, face-to-face with her son, in broad daylight.

This vision, as Vronskaya had crassly predicted, pierced Sergei's heart like a poisoned dart. It literally made him sick: he developed a fever much like the one he'd had seventeen months earlier, when Anna had come to visit for his birthday.

On that occasion, when Anna Karenina surprised him, Sergei hadn't been afraid at all; even if they had told him his mother was dead, he wouldn't have believed them; he could feel it, he knew it, he was certain that "death doesn't exist." That day, his birthday, she was there when he awoke, sitting on the edge of his bed, alive, whole, gazing at him, loving him.

But when her portrait appeared, even if they had tried to hide the fact that she was no longer alive, he would have felt that she was dead, he *knew* it. In the light of day, against all logic, she had appeared. Luminous, the most beautiful, most perfect—most feared and most desired—of all ghosts, there in front of him, in the street, about to enter his house. . . .

Rescued from obscurity in 1905, Mikhailov's portrait of Anna is neither the reappearance of a ghost nor the incarnation of death. Claudia looks at it while the servants dust it off and hang it where a landscape used to hang on a wall in Sergei's office: she's no expert, but to her it looks like the canvas is the master-work of some fictional painter.

30. About Clementine

Let's try to retrace Clementine's steps back to the day when Vronskaya played her little trick, exposing Karenina's portrait to the elements and piercing Sergei's heart. Like a poisoned dart from far-off lands, decorated with feathers for a momentous occasion, crafted with great skill, it's not the decoration that makes the portrait great, but its accuracy—if the dart flies well and hits its target, it's because of the restraint with which it captures beauty; the precision of its flight is assured by the painting's painstaking execution, the components that compose that beauty are what allow it to fly true, tracing the fine arc of perfection. The dart and the portrait are finely wrought but weightless.

(We might ask why on earth miserable old Mikhailov, of all people—everyone knows he's not a great man, he's jealous and disparaging of others, a total stranger to sympathy and compassion, an egotist—had the genius to create such a masterpiece? Although he lacked any moral qualities, he had been given a gift. What kind of dart might we compare him to? Or is it the case that the artist is the opposite of the dart, and what makes it fly so well are the defects in his personality, the ugliness of his character?)

But back to Clementine. Her history is a patchwork of scraps from various workshops. She was raised among seamstresses, sewing from the age of four or five—under duress—in the company of other seamstresses' children. She was cut from good cloth, unlike Mikhailov; she made a first-class sail, capable of withstanding stormy winds. And unlike Mikhailov, she was never an opportunist, never put her own interests first, and was never motivated by jealousy, ill will, or contempt.

For our purposes, what matters is that Clementine has no one to share her memories, to treasure her past, because her mother died young, and she never knew her father. When she was twelve, she got her own workbench because she was so skilled, and she had a grandmother and two little brothers who would show up asking for money; they were her responsibility, one she assumed without complaint. After all, they were her flesh and blood and the source of her strength. But they didn't last long; age and illness quickly did away with them.

Not long thereafter, Clementine organized the whole workshop—all the seamstresses, and without putting her needle down—to fight for their rights. She linked up with the heads of other workshops. By the time she was fourteen, the police had come to pay her a visit and taken her away. That's when she met Vladimir.

Vladimir's a different story. As a child he was a watchmaker's assistant. Later he became a footman, but the church priest wanted him to be able to make a decent living. So instead of serving a nobleman, he serves Gapon. He's his confidante, messenger, scribe (he learned to read and write as a boy, with the aforementioned priest), deputy, a jack-of-all-trades. When Clementine, the leader of the seamstresses, was about to be eaten alive by the tsar's people, the organization defended her; she was a great leader, and she was a woman. Vladimir was her contact; that's how they met. Vladimir is the feather to Clementine's dart, giving her life stability, meaning. He keeps her on the straight and narrow. He puts wind in her sails. He makes her fly true.

But Aleksandra's death has changed Vladimir. He's no longer a jack-of-all-trades. He's no longer satisfied with being the feather on a dart, a mere adornment. He wants to be a dart himself, or a sword, or a bullet. He begins plotting with Clementine.

31. The Critics Examine the Portrait

Three months after Bloody Sunday—things move slowly at the palace—James Schmidt, the assistant to the curator at the Hermitage, is the first to come and see the portrait of Anna Karenina. He examines the canvas in silence, but he can't hide his enthusiasm. When Claudia reports back to Sergei (omitting his visible enthusiasm, which is not a lie because Schmidt didn't say one word), her husband thinks, *They won't buy it,* and is relieved. He still finds the idea that the painting might be exhibited repugnant.

The Hermitage sends a second visitor, artist and curator Ernest Liphart, but not immediately—as mentioned, things at the palace are moving slowly and inefficiently, paralyzing the institutions that rely on it. Perhaps because of the climate—it's springtime already—Sergei likes the idea of speaking with him. And because he's familiar with Liphart's portraits and paintings, Sergei thinks the canvas won't be of any interest to him; courtly art is not his cup of tea.

They invite him to dine. Sergei and his guest chat about opera, they're both ardent enthusiasts, and Claudia discusses costume design with him.

After their postprandial chat, Claudia takes him to see Mikhailov's painting, and Liphart waxes lyrical about its many charms.

The third visit occurs shortly thereafter. It's Ivan Vsevolozhsky, director of the Hermitage, who says nothing, goes directly about his business, and leaves after examining the portrait for a long while.

All three visitors are extremely keen. They note the painting's unique features, its technical perfection, and its understanding of the model; they compare it (both verbally and in their written communications with the tsar) to Tolstoy's novel, declaring the portrait to be superior. The painter's psychological understanding of his subject and his vision are so deep that there's nothing in the portrait that doesn't express the woman herself. . . . When Ivan Vsevolozhsky gives his opinion, he says that when he first set eyes on the painting, his initial thought was, "Get up and walk!"

One other person asks to come and see it: Vsevolozhsky's wife, Ekaterina Dmitrievna, née Volkonsky. Because she's not involved in the negotiations and has nothing to hide, she bursts into tears when she sees it. She doesn't say a single word. The next day she sends a gift hamper decorated with cut flowers to the Karenins. It's full of sweets and delicacies that Claudia sends immediately to Anya in another container, because the basket is just too lovely and the flowers that decorate it make three arrangements for the table. Claudia makes a smaller one, which she wraps in purple paper, and sends it over to Anya that same day.

After the four visits, no one else comes. The functionaries have too many things to do, or at least they should. But the idea of acquiring the canvas isn't lost in the shuffle. At the end of May, the Karenins receive a letter informing them that the painting will become part of the imperial collection in the second week of June; it will be taken directly to the museum and payment will follow immediately. The no-strings-attached, free money is much more than Sergei and Claudia had expected.

"Shouldn't we tell Anya about the sale, Sergei? Strictly speaking, it belongs to both of you."

"Legally speaking it's mine."

"I said strictly speaking."

"You brought the portraits of my mother here because you knew that Anya had absolutely no interest in them. She's more my father's child than I am. She doesn't even remember. . . ."

Sergei never mentions his mother, not even by her name, those two familiar syllables.

"But she had no idea how valuable the painting was. It's a very expensive piece. . . . We don't need the money."

"That wasn't what you said when you convinced me to sell the painting."

"You know Anya lives from hand to mouth."

"Don't worry about that. We'll settle up by paying for repairs on the Karenin Palace, they're becoming more urgent every day."

The Karenin Palace has fallen into disrepair without the attentions of Kapitonich, who awaits his departure for the other world in his bed in the servants' quarters, refusing all visitors. The cook sends Valeria up with his food, but she can't stand the old man; she pushes the plates at him like he's a dog.

"Sergei, if you give her—"

"Out of the question. You know I pay the servants, including the new hall porter. And you pay for her food and her clothes."

"Fine, fine. I wasn't asking about that. I thought it was a nice idea. I was going to ask about inviting her to dinner. So we can give her the news."

"Absolutely not. Don't even think about it."

The portrait's sale has awakened Sergei's childhood demon—jealousy—and he has no desire to rein it in. Anya, along with Vronsky, stole his mother. Nothing, not a thing for her. He hated having to pay for her needs—but he knew that, when it came down to it, she was completely dependent on him because it was his prerogative, a fact he was more keenly aware of than ever, now that he was taking his sweet time to reconcile the accounts. The truth is, it wasn't in his interest to give Anya "her" money. If he gave her the amount designated in his father's will, Anya would receive a monthly stipend similar to what she got from Sergei. But he wasn't about to, and he was under no obligation, because according to the will, she had to marry to receive the stipend. And Anya will never marry.

It both irritates and pleases Sergei to make his sister dependent on him. Anya is financially tied to the Karenins; she's their household dependent.

32. Vladimir

When Vladimir is confronted with Aleksandra's death, it takes over his whole world. He can't bear losing his sister. A part of him dies with her. But Clementine saves him, amongst the dead. She takes him on a walk through the cemetery of the Holy Transfiguration Cathedral (at Preobrazhensky on the south-eastern outskirts of the city) while she tells him in detail about the demonstration on Bloody Sunday, what the Cossacks did, what happened to Volodin and the others who died that day, and what has happened since. She takes him to the corner of the cemetery, where the police dumped three-dozen cadavers in a mass grave on January 10, no coffins for them, just sacks of cloth, "like hams."

"If they had taken Aleksandra to the Obukhov Hospital, like most of the seriously wounded and dead, she'd be here, with my friend Volodin. You knew him too. I hear he died because he wanted to look after Aleksandra when that imbecile Father Gapon made her march. These are your brothers, Vladimir, every one of them. We must fight for them. They didn't take just your only sister—as you told me—they took something more, from all of us. They took away our Russia. They want to devour it. We have to resist, to fight them, seize it from their hands before nothing's left of it, not even a hint of life. Aleksandra was prop-erly buried and mourned. But they want to take these rights—to be mourned, to have siblings, to live—away from every last one of us, they want to bury us in common graves when we've expended our usefulness. Enough! No more! No more!"

The state's crime was "beyond measure"; they had killed defenseless people, many more than those that lay there "tossed in a hole without any respect, like animals." But "neither you nor I nor anyone capable of feeling will allow their sacrifice to be made in vain. They fell, but their deaths will be the beginning of the end for this corrupt regime. Vladimir, there are children here, women, and the elderly too. Do you see? They want to make Russia a slaughterhouse. They eat, drink, and celebrate, paying for their luxuries with the lives of our people. They'll turn all of Russia into a common grave. Enough! No more! No more!"

"You and I, Vladimir, what we should be doing is eating the rich. Let's go eat the rich!"

33. The Reason for the Proposed Purchase

It wasn't the caliber of the painting or the notoriety of its subject that prompted the portrait's inclusion in the imperial collection. The painter has become wildly popular and acquired immense prestige. He's esteemed by friends and enemies alike. It's only natural that they'd be scouring the earth and the heavens for more of his work.

This sudden wave of interest in the artist was started by another Mikhailov, a somewhat high-ranking functionary in the Special Corps (formerly the Okhrana, or secret police), the son and sole heir of Mikhailov the artist. He's the one who's been pulling strings to create interest in his father's work, with the sole intention of elevating its price. That's why he's been instigating the acquisition of some of his paintings, and that's how the portrait of Anna Karenina came to receive so much attention. When all is said and done, the son is a good policeman, but not a reader—he hasn't read *Anna Karenina*, not a single one of Tolstoy's works (this is worth mentioning in passing, though it's not a critical point); in general, he doesn't give a damn when it comes to art in any form. His wallet, on the other hand . . .

But the things Mikhailov has done out of greed, are they the reason for the wild enthusiasm of the renowned museum director and his pair of critics? Have they been influenced by the wave of popularity the artist's work is enjoying? Have they been swayed by the market? If that were the case, how could we explain the fact that the director's good-hearted wife, Ekaterina Dmitrievna, melted like snow in the sun when she set eyes on the canvas?

Let's be very careful here. The root cause of the artist's prestige is greed, wheeling and dealing, of that there's no question. But the roots must belong to a tree, or at the very least a blade of grass, which was born from a seed. And the seed is Tolstoy's novel, his description of the portrait's grandeur: *It was not a picture, but a living and charming woman with curly black hair, bare shoulders and arms, and a dreamy half-smile.*

Mikhailov's apologists might say that the earth in which this seed was planted is even more important than its Tolstoyan origins, and they'd argue that the painting itself is of great worth, that the canvas has its own intrinsic value. And yet . . .

34. The Portrait Departs

It's the night of June 14, 1905. In the morning, they'll come for the portrait by Mikhailov, to take it for installation at the museum, for the exhibit dedicated to the aforementioned artist. Anya now knows; Claudia told her. She reacted violently— furious, obsessive, confused, so irritating that even Claudia lost her patience. Anya refuses to see her brother or her sister-in-law, yet she inundates them with letters full of contradictory messages. Which is why husband and wife, asleep in their separate bedrooms, both have the same dream:

Someone arrives at the door of the house; they assume it's another letter from Anya. "I'll have to go and see her," Claudia says to herself, "to convince her not to make such a mountain out of a molehill." Sergei says to himself, "I should have prevented things from coming to this." They're both thinking of Anya—Claudia's worrying about what to say and what gift to bring on her visit; Sergei is filled with a brotherly love he never feels in real life—when Leo Tolstoy enters the parlor. He barges in, roaring at the top of his lungs, "I want a world without violence, power, or government. . . . Government is always corrupt; it uses violence, both real and imaginary, to retain power." Tolstoy realizes he's standing in front of Sergei and Claudia, greeting them curtly—"Madame Claudia Karenina"—and continues:

"There's no time to delay the reason for my visit with pleasantries. Where is Sergei? I need to talk to him."

Sergei:

"That's me." He notices Tolstoy's confusion and elaborates. "I'm Sergei Karenin."

"You . . . ? You? Yes, of course; I didn't recognize you, what was I thinking . . . ? You weren't a child forever. . . . I always think of you as a boy, Sergei, occasionally as a young man who has just begun to sprout a beard. Let me get straight to the point: the gravity of the situation obliges me to make this visit. You can't let Anna Karenina's portrait end up in the tsar's hands, he's a foolish man who's his own worst enemy, and he's an enemy of the common good, to boot. You just can't give it to him. That fellow Mikhailov painted her at *my* behest. *I'm* the author. I don't like saying so—I have no interest whatsoever in staking my claim, I abhor all forms of private property—but you have no right to hand over something that I—"

Claudia has been listening serenely. Wisely, she interrupts him when she knows that doing so will ease his anxiety:

"We understand, we have no doubts that the marvelous canvas is your creation and that Sergei is *your* character. . . ."

"That's quite enough, Claudia," Tolstoy says. "You have less right than anyone to speak. . . . Only a woman or a doctor could utter such drivel! What an insult, his own wife . . . !"

Sergei intervenes, mastering his nature, in a calm, clear voice:

"It's absolutely true. Hard to swallow and even harder to for me, even for us, to comprehend, but it's the truth."

His words make the author explode:

"Enough, enough! Not another word. I *found* you, Sergei, don't you see? You were there, I saw you, and I made you visible to others. Our relationship is the same as Mikhailov's to the creature in the portrait, no more and no less. I'm no God, no creator. I'm just a man, and I don't even know if I'm a good one. I want to be a good man. Family, friends, and love are far more valuable and more important than writing millions of words. When you take action, you know if you succeed, and if you fail, you can change your course. But if you write, then what? How do you know whether your audience understands you, whether you move them, whether they care? But it doesn't matter! What matters is the common good. What matters is that we can't allow the portrait of Anna Karenina to fall into the tsar's hands. It's unacceptable! But I'm not the one to stand and fight this battle, I would look like a megalomaniac, and I'm not! I'm not the one at stake! Listen to me! Try to understand! The fate of the canvas lies in your hands, both of yours. Sergei, do you understand what you're giving away? Do you realize how the tsar will profit from it? How do you think that makes me feel? Just try and imagine. If paying taxes is tantamount to financing murders, this is much more serious than paying taxes. You'll get money from the tsar, and in exchange you'll give him your past, your own past, your roots, you're giving away your own mother!" Tolstoy erupts, screaming and brandishing his fist in Sergei's face. "You self-absorbed, self-serving fool!"

Tolstoy takes a few steps; the reception hall is larger in their dreams, huge like the tsarina's, and his strides are so gigantic it's hard to take him seriously.

Here, the dreams of husband and wife diverge. In Sergei's dream, a fireplace is lit. In Claudia's, it's not. Tolstoy recovers his composure in both dreams:

"You're accepting money the tsar has taken from the Russian people to feed and grow his death machine. And you're giving him something pure, unsullied, unique, priceless in exchange for that money. You can't allow it. Not on my account. This wouldn't matter if it were a question of arrogance or pride—if that were the case I wouldn't be here. I urge you in the name of all that's worthy in mankind. Consider it carefully. It's not right. It's steeped in evil. It's affirming a reign of murder and violence. There's no need to go into detail, let's stick to the basics: commanding an army is neither honorable nor important, but they have the tyrant's ear and tell him that it is, the flatterers. It's shameful to organize killings. An army is always an instrument of murder, and in the case of the tsar's army, it's also a suicide machine—Russia is killing itself."

Tolstoy has yet to sit down, but in Claudia's and Sergei's dreams he gets out of his chair—according to that dream logic in which you can see someone go up and down stairs to the same landing (it could never happen on stairs made of brick and mortar, but in dreams those stairs can lead to the same landing, a metaphor for life).

In both Claudia's and Sergei's dreams, the writer looks askance at the room that Claudia has decorated with such care. He sees it with a novelist's eye. He thinks of what he wrote in *The Death of Ivan Ilyich*, "In reality it was just what is usually seen in the houses of people of moderate means who want to appear rich, and therefore succeed only in resembling others like themselves: there are damasks, dark wood, plants, rugs, and dull and polished bronzes—all the things people of a certain class have in order to resemble other people of that class." Then he regards the room with his essayist's eye, and he feels even more disdain, but it's what he sees with his moralist's eye that makes Count Leo Tolstoy feel profound disgust.

"I don't know what I'm doing here. I can't afford to waste any more time. I'm an old man, and it's clear that my pleas are falling on deaf ears. I know all too well that people of your class—and I'm responsible for ensconcing you in it, Sergei—lead their lives with their own interests at heart. You build your lives on foundations of pride, cruelty, violence, and evil. But what I have created—and there is no trace of me in this unholy business—and what I cannot take responsibility for, is that the two of you are not acknowledging change, you don't so much as lift a finger. You've become increasingly self-absorbed, ruining yourselves, and, I won't deny it, you disgust me. Your complacency will cause you nothing but unhappiness, and me, pain. Man cannot live without knowing the truth, not even if he's a man of fiction, not even the fiction I write, because I write only what I know, and the only world I know is that of men."

"If you give us an order, we'll obey it." The connection between an author and his character is unique, unlike any other bond. Sergei says this because he understands Tolstoy's disgust, and he sympathizes with him.

"Terrible, the custom of giving orders! There's nothing more perverse, nothing that corrupts sensible and healthy social order more than such 'orders.' Imposing directions on people as if they were sheep! On no condition will I give you an order! I'm appealing to your better sides, and that's it! I won't respond by doing something that would disgust me even further! No, I don't give orders, and I don't keep slaves. I'm trying to appeal to your ethical sides, to your better selves."

In Claudia's dream, she exchanges glances with Sergei. In Sergei's dream, they don't. But in both dreams, Sergei reflects:

"But I'm not completely human. And you know that better than anyone: I'm a fictional creation, part of an imaginary drama. I'm your invention. You're responsible for my existence. All my actions are determined by you. They're not orders, they're something more than that. I'm a puppet, I . . ."

This statement infuriates Tolstoy, who roars at the top of his lungs:

"You are what you are, Sergei! Just as whole as I am, as much of a person as the rest of us. Don't try to pin something that has nothing to do with me on me!"

"But I'm not. Let's end this charade."

"The proof is in the pudding. For example: I can't stand the opera. You and your little sister adore it."

The elderly writer doesn't mask his rage. Sergei doesn't give in. In his dream, he stammers:

"I'm made of i-i-i-ink. A puppet made of ink!"

In Claudia's dream, he doesn't stammer, and he says something else:

"Most people live as if they're walking backward toward a cliff. They know that behind them there's an abyss they could fall into any moment, but they pretend to ignore it and keep looking at the scenery. But I don't walk. You created me in the abyss of nonexistence."

In both dreams, Tolstoy responds, screaming:

"That's completely untrue."

And Sergei replies calmly:

"Only subconscious action is productive, and the individual who plays a role in historical events never understands this. If he tries to understand, he's punished with sterility."

"Enough, Sergei, enough! Stop quoting me! Be reasonable. . . ."

The old man watches them in silence for a few moments, then he says, looking first at Claudia, then at Sergei:

"Don't you realize? Just as the French were called to renew the world in 1790, we Russians are being called to do so in 1905."

"I disagree," Sergei says. "If it were the case that human beings were governed by reason, there would be no such thing as life."

"So what? So what! Stop quoting me back to myself!" Tolstoy tries to contain an outburst of rage, repeating the following words as quietly as he can in his agitated state: "They're making me despise myself. This is sinful, to get angry at my very own work. I'm destroying the bonds of love. And the wound bleeds. . . ." Once again, Tolstoy takes a few giant strides in the room that has grown ever larger in both dreams. And he says aloud, though much more calmly, "Because you and I, Sergei, are joined only by a bond of love. That's all. Which is why our relations are so volatile. The wound bleeds, it bleeds. . . ."

As he pronounces these last words, in both Sergei's dream and Claudia's, Tolstoy turns into something like a fox, and immediately thereafter into something like a hedgehog, changing shape and size from one animal to another.

That's when Claudia awakens, the final words of her dream echoing: "The wound bleeds, it bleeds. . . ."

Sergei continues sleeping; his dreams veer off into other characters and absurd scenarios that he won't remember (like a fox hunt in which the horses are ridden by hedgehogs), obliterating his encounter with his author. His dream becomes more straightforward and easy to follow. Then it vanishes in smoke.

35. Between the Dream and the Battleship Potemkin

While Sergei's dream begins to fragment into different images, far away in the Black Sea, on board the Battleship Potemkin, an ill-tempered, disrespectful officer whose name no one wants to recall sparks a fire. There are several versions of this story.

According to the popular one, the officer who lit the match was walking among the hammocks where his men were sleeping, completely disregarding the crew's precious personal space. Rudely, he disrupted their sleep.

According to some who adhere to this version, he deliberately bumped into a handsome young sailor (Ivan); according to others who believe this story, it was involuntary, an accident.

Some swear that the officer wasn't high-ranking and that he went down to the crew's quarters with the express intention of visiting a young man (Ivan) with whom he had been having his way, and young Ivan, the object of his desire, wanted to get rid of him and raised the alarm.

As the story goes, in the middle of the night an officer awakens a sailor, exhausted from his long workday. The gravelly voice of another crew member, Vakulenchuk, galvanizes the others to take action against the transgressor.

"Comrades, it's time to make a move."

He makes a little speech (neither as long nor as moving as Father Gapon's, it's improvised and has a touch of fury that the reverend's didn't when we heard him speak that Saturday). When he finishes, the sailors respond in unison, as if they've rehearsed.

"We're not gonna eat rotten stew anymore."

The instigator, Vakulenchuk, starts speaking again, invigorated by their unanimous reply.

"The Japanese feed their Russian prisoners better!"

Only one of the sailors on the Potemkin, Matyushenko, a deep sleeper, remains in Morpheus's arms, though he's not completely oblivious to what's going on. He's dreaming of Claudia. Perhaps he doesn't recognize her in his dream, but he knows her well; Matyushenko is the husband of the young woman who works for Anya, Valeria, the one who wants to know how to avoid having children. Claudia is telling him, "Sailors should take a vow not to eat."

She's sitting at a table that looks like it's made of glass, laden with plates and glasses and glass bottles, too, overflowing with food and drink. She takes a spoonful (he can't see what it is because the spoon isn't made of glass) and puts it in her mouth, continuing to speak while she splatters him with food. "You should renounce it, sailor. All sailors who are going to sea should renounce food!"

Claudia eats and eats, spewing food; the sailor feels an uncontrollable desire to grab the spoon from her and devour the food. When he tries to, a fence of huge knives springs up between them, their sharp points facing him. But young Matyushenko is oblivious to danger: he's mad with hunger.

As soon as he takes a step toward the fence of pointed knives, the fear of impaling himself awakens him; he becomes conscious of his hunger and the surrounding commotion of his shipmates, who are starving like him, and all worked up, as we've seen.

36. Claudia's Regrets

At the same time, in Sergei and Claudia's house, in the room next to Sergei's, Claudia lies in bed thinking, *It's my fault, mine. I'm the one who convinced Sergei to sell the portrait of his mother. I'm the one who's giving the painting of Tolstoy's character to the tsar. Sergei didn't want to. I, I . . . Am I reprehensible? Everything appears different now from how it did when we accepted. . . . Our Russia is a different country. . . .*

She tries to calm down by telling herself, *What Tolstoy said was just a dream, this wouldn't matter a fig to him.* But it doesn't calm her; it doesn't work. *According to Lantur* (the cook), *dreams speak truth. . . . Enough! She's the cook, what does she know? . . . But she's right, she's right.*

She tries not to think, to go to sleep. In the anxiety of this unfamiliar insomnia, her remorse is eating away at her. Claudia gets out of bed, takes her lamp, and goes downstairs to Sergei's study.

She enters his study and lights three bright lamps, which illuminate the portrait in all its splendor. The magnificent, lovely Anna Karenina, never more beautiful, is the sun at midnight. Claudia has her back to it because of the way the lamps are positioned. She's still holding the base of the third lamp when she sees the box covered in blue cloth, which she found next to the portrait in the attic, on a stool next to the chair of Sergei's desk.

"How could I have forgotten about this," she says to herself. "I haven't laid eyes on it since I brought it down from the attic."

She picks up the box and puts it on the desk. She undoes the ribbon, tied in a bow that keeps it shut. Once white, it has yellowed over the years. When she unties it, its different shades are visible.

"This ribbon has seen better days, it's been marking time. . . ."

Inside the box is the manuscript that Anna Karenina wrote when she was at her very happiest. Beautifully bound in leather, it submits to Claudia's touch. She takes it out, places it on the desk, and sets her lamp nearby to read. Then she sees there's another manuscript at the bottom of the box, thinner and written in a smaller script on loose sheets. On the first page, she reads:

> Seryozha, my son: I will never deserve your forgiveness. Nothing in my life ever compared to being your mother. I will always love you, wherever I am. I wrote this novel twice. The first I wrote as a moral lesson for children, intending that you be its first reader. Two years later, I rewrote it in one sitting, without any such pretentions. I didn't write it for you. I wrote it for myself. Nevertheless, I dedicate it to you, hoping that someday you, Seryozha, will have a daughter, and that one day, she'll be a grown woman, and these pages will speak to her, my granddaughter, when she's an adult. My love . . .

The last sentence is unfinished. The signature is incomplete, and unnecessary.

Claudia sits down in Sergei's comfortable armchair. She chooses the unbound manuscript, Anna's book, Karenina's novel. . . .

37. In Claudia's Hands

In her hands, Claudia holds the loose leaves of Anna's book. They're bound together by a simple, utilitarian ribbon that's not as nice as the one that fastened the blue box, thick and coarse material, undyed. When she unties it, a calling card printed with Count Vronsky's name falls out, the typeface elegant and restrained, with a few handwritten lines:

> I often fell into a dreamlike state on opium; I stood at the window on summer nights, watching the sea and the city without moving, absorbed by all I saw, from the time the sun rose until night fell . . . T. de Q.

PART FOUR

THE BOOK OF ANNA

♕

No date or place

38. An Opium-Infused Fairy Tale:
The Book of Anna by Anna Karenina

Once upon a time, a woodsman and his wife lived deep in the forest with their six-year-old daughter, Anna. Theirs was a hard life, and their daughter was their only joy. It had been a long winter, and there was little food for the table, yet the girl laughed, impervious to hunger, cold, the dark, and her parents' constant ill humor.

One day before sunrise, the woodsman (who never laughed, just like his wife) leaves the cottage and begins to walk, cutting a gaunt, disagreeable figure, his axe and some rope in his hands. He knows his search is in vain. The birds and the ducks have all flown south; the bears, the snakes, the wildcats, and even the creepy-crawlies are all hidden away, settled down for a long winter's nap; the fish hide beneath the ice. His memory leads him to a path, and there he glimpses something in the pale light of the moon, which also looks frozen.

The woodsman takes stiff steps; his head is heavy, as if it's filled with cold water. A light breaks the darkness, so bright that he can no longer see the path. *Could it be the reflection off the blade of my axe? How is that possible?* he asks himself silently. He's so cold inside that he can no longer think clearly. He recalls old tales of men who lost their minds because of their weapons. Instinctively he moves the axe in his hand, but the light doesn't change. He lifts his face to the sky, eyeing the splendorous light, but can't see a thing; the moon has been outshone, no longer visible. Then he thinks, *The stars have all died.*

Light that obliterates all other light is dangerous, but this thought doesn't occur to the woodsman. Neither does he think of the sky as black velvet; he was born poor.

He waits a little while for his eyes to adjust. At risk of getting lost, he stumbles in the direction of the shining light. It's coming from a woman dressed in iridescent blue satin, sparks flying from her fingernails and teeth, her hair filaments of light. She opens her mouth to speak and he sees the source of the light inside her mouth.

"I know your daughter is hungry. Why let an innocent girl suffer when I can help you? Bring her to me, and I will look after her and protect her."

Sparks fly with each of her words, accompanied by a clap of thunder.

The woodsman backs away without saying a word, without taking his eyes off the woman. She opens her mouth wider, like she's yawning, and even more light pours forth. She's lit up from inside. When he reaches the path, the Illuminata fades into darkness silently. It takes some time for the woodsman to get his bearings. In the sky he sees the far-off splendor of the rising sun, which means his home must be somewhere to the right. So he goes left, brandishing his axe, declaring, "I'm going to find something to eat. I'm hungry!"

A pair of eyes blink at him, knee-high. The woodsman lifts his axe. The eyes regard him; they belong to an animal—though he can't see what kind—who says calmly (and without an accent), "You'll get only one meal out of me. Feed me to your wife and daughter. I'll be the last thing you eat this winter. You'll die of hunger. Don't be a fool, give your daughter to the Illuminata."

The animal laughs the same laugh as the woodsman's daughter. Although the creature's words paralyze the woodsman and its laugh terrifies him, he lets his axe fall on his prey. Hunger trumps fear. The animal's warm blood spatters the woodsman's face. He trusses its legs with his rope without noting what kind of animal it is and begins to return home with his quarry.

His wife and Anna both receive him, clapping with joy (and with cold). The girl laughs, the same laugh that was the animal's final utterance. The woodsman shuts his eyes and the girl, like her mother, thinks it's because he's tired and his belly is empty. The mother begins to prepare the creature for stewing. Anna wipes her father's face, wetting the edge of her skirt with his water jug and rinsing it afterward, singing, "Finally we have some food on the fire. . . ."

The girl sings and, as if it's part of her song, she laughs. And each time she laughs, the woodsman's blood grows colder.

The threesome sits at the table. When the hunter is served his stew, he doesn't take a single bite. He can't eat the creature whose eyes he looked into, who foretold a future of grief. He recalls the animal's words: "You'll all die of hunger." Anna laughs. The man cries.

The woman and the girl eat; they're so happy to have food that they don't even realize the woodsman is crying. He thinks, *My wife is going to eat me, because grief will kill me before hunger does.* Before they finish their servings, he wipes his eyes, closes them, and doesn't open them again until the table has been cleared.

When Anna falls asleep, the woodsman tells his wife every-thing about his two encounters. She makes up her mind.

"We must not eat any more of this meat you've brought home. Not you, not I, not Anna. We have no way of knowing it's not the meat of Evil. And you should take the girl to the woman of light. I have no doubt she's the Virgin—she's the only one who has an internal light—and that Our Lady will look after her, and once this horrible winter has ended, we'll see her again. She'll bring her back to us, happy and healthy."

"That woman can't possibly be divine. If you could only see the light when she speaks, you feel . . ."

The woodsman can't express how this woman's words shine like jewels that have been extracted from a mine with the sweat and toil of mankind, because he's never laid eyes on such jew-els; he doesn't even know what a mine is or where to find one—if he had, he'd never forget the jewels' glitter; he's a woods-man. If he knew where to find a mine or knew that precious stones could be polished, he would have gone and asked for a job; digging and polishing would be preferable to dying of hunger, and blackening his lungs would be better than being stewed without salt by his own wife.

"Give her our girl. She's the Virgin, she knows all. Give her our daughter, but don't tell her her name. If she's not the Virgin, she won't be able to call her Anna, and our daughter will come back and find us, because no one can live without hearing their own name."

"But . . . but . . ." It's impossible for the woodsman to explain what he wants to say.

"All right?" she says, seeing him babble like a poor fool. "Take Anna before we get hungry again, because I won't give her any more of that meat you brought us. I'll throw it away in the hollow, where the wolves can eat it."

Before dawn, the woodsman leaves the cottage, Anna asleep in his arms. He heads in the same direction as the previous day, but before his feet become stiff with cold, the bright light appears, the Illuminata behind it. The radiance awakens the girl; she laughs (as she always does) at the sight of the Illuminata and reaches out to her; the Illuminata embraces her, and they disappear. The light fades.

The grayness of the day falls on the woodsman, a heavy burden.

He walks home. He's so overcome, he doesn't hear the wolves howling, the ones who ate the stew his wife threw away in the hollow during the night. They don't howl like normal wolves; they seem to speak, and the sound of what they say is terrifying.

The woodsman cannot sleep. He can't even think about his daughter. His only thought is that his wife is going to eat him, that his body will end up on a plate at his own table, that his wife will sing, *Finally we have some food on the fire* as she stews him.

He thinks his wife will serve three portions on three plates—
one for her husband, the second for her daughter, and the third
for herself—and she'll devour them all because hunger will have
warped her soul.

From the day she arrives at the Illuminata's palace, the girl
dresses in velvet, and in the summer she wears satin, silk, and
lace. She learns the names of these fabrics and how to judge
threads and brocades. She is taught to sew, to embroider, to sing,
and to write. She is called Forest Girl. She's given a personal
servant, Maslova. She's never hungry; she even forgets what it's
like to feel hungry, and she forgets how to laugh the way she used
to in her parents' cottage.

The Illuminata lives in a wing of the enormous palace where
the girl is forbidden to go. An entire year passes, and then
another, and then ten more. One of these years the girl forgets
the cottage and the forest. She can no longer recall her mother's
face or hear her voice. She has a vague memory of her father
from dreaming about him, but she can't see him clearly, not
even in her dreams. In another year, he disappears from her
memory too. And in another year, she forgets the name she
was given at birth, and how to laugh. Her face, expressionless
and austere, has become the face of a beautiful woman, as has
her body.

In the forest that surrounds her parents' cottage (which she never
thinks of any longer), the wolves who devoured huge mouthfuls
of the stew made from the unidentifiable creature laugh night
and day, the same laugh as the girl, mimicking what they heard
when the Illuminata first met the woodsman—sheer evil.

Some might say that the girl in our story is not living in paradise: she has lost her loved ones, and all she has left is her
Maslova—but even she disappears from the story, mentioned
in passing only a few times. The girl had a deep bond with her

father—poor man!—and her mother, too (after all, they had both eaten the stew made from the talking animal), whereas with the Illuminata there's not even a trace of affection. Before, all she had was the laugh that quickly became frightening; now, she has everything, but there are no commas, no periods, no parentheses, nothing to fill her mouth, her heart, her soul but a jumble of words.

Others, however, might say that the girl has enviable good fortune, because she wants for nothing. Thanks to the art of magic, she has gone from famine to feast; from poverty to a life in a palace so huge she still hasn't explored it all; from washing her father's face with her own skirt to having lots of dresses and plenty of servants to wait on her.

Early one morning, the Illuminata, who still calls her Forest Girl, says, "I'm going on a journey. I'm going to give you the key chain for my wing in the palace. You may use all my rooms, read all my books, touch all my things, and eat whatever you like. There are only three locks, and I'm giving you the three keys that open them. The first is for the door that connects this part of the palace to mine, the second is the key to the room where I keep my jewels, and the third should not be opened under any circumstances. You may explore wherever you wish, but not that last room, which you'll recognize by its purple door. This is the key. I'm leaving it in your care as well. But I repeat: do not use it, or you will risk losing everything."

The enormous key is covered in shiny leather, and though it has teeth, it looks strange because it is curved in places. Nothing the Forest Girl has ever seen looks like the key, which hangs from the Illuminata's chain with two others.

No sooner does she finish giving her instructions than the Illuminata leaves. Without hesitation, the Forest Girl puts a key in the first door and passes through it. Before she has a chance to take in her surroundings, the servants (none of whom she recognizes) offer her sweets and food, then take her into another room where there is a huge table replete with delicacies.

The girl sits at the head of the table. The footmen light the candles. The rooms in this wing of the palace are much darker than her own; heavy curtains cover the windows, blocking out all sunlight.

The first dish is a meat stew. She doesn't think she recognizes the flavor of the meat, but she likes it very much, and when she finishes, she's certain that she's tasted it before. While she eats, they pour her wine, and she tries alcohol for the first time. They offer her vodka, but she declines. They bring more dishes, which she recognizes neither the scent nor the flavor of, and she declines these as well.

The wine animates her. She explores more rooms in the company of numerous servants. She smiles; it's been a very long time since she has, and she looks different than when she was a girl. She laughs, but it's not her laugh, it's hardly audible, there's something tinny about it, like the workings of a clock or watch. The footmen drag her around, showing her paintings and other objects in the room, telling her about each canvas, showing her how to use the objects—what they do and how to play with them. They're both servants and teachers.

They come to the door with the second lock, but the girl isn't the least bit curious ("Why would I want to look at jewels when I'm already surrounded by them?") and they pass it by. Each room leads to more rooms. They come to the third door, gigantic and purple. The servants don't say a word. The Forest Girl remembers the Illuminata's instructions, shrugs her shoulders, and—always accompanied by servants—retraces her steps. In the next room, they offer her more sweets and libations. She laughs once more—her clockwork laugh—and her smile is frozen on her face, as if it has been painted there permanently.

She uses the first key again to return to the other side of the palace. She retires to her room. It's just past noon, but she lies down on her bed and falls into a deep sleep. She dreams of her parents. This dream wipes the smile from her face. She's troubled when she awakens, though she's unsure why, trying not to remember what she's just seen so clearly in her dream.

She jumps out of bed. The sun is setting. Once again, she passes through the door to the other side of the palace. She's offered sweets, candies, and wine—a rainbow of colors—but she declines them all. She snoops around. She's fascinated by the visible workings of a grandfather clock and begins to laugh without realizing that she and the clock sound remarkably similar; she contemplates an oil painting of a naked youth lying in front of a bearded old man.

The youth extends a hand, trying to reach the old man in vain. The Forest Girl feels sad and then angry. "Why doesn't he get up? Why is he lying there like a newborn babe? Why is it so hard for him to stand on his own two legs? Why doesn't the youth pull himself up by the old man's beard?"

In the room that is also the library, the books sit next to things on the shelves. There is a bottle next to a spine that reads *The Genie in the Bottle*. A globe rests atop *A Treatise on Geography*. A little wooden chest sits next to *The Treasure Chest*. There's a spinning wheel next to *Sleeping Beauty*. *The Prince* and a tiny crown. *Cinderella* and a little gold slipper. She sits down to read a book with an absurd title: *Theme without Language*. The clocks mark the hours' passage. Trays with food and sweets circulate. "They want to stupefy me with excess. But I won't let them. I'm going to see everything, everything."

Late that night the Forest Girl returns; in the butler's pantry off the kitchen, she eats a slice of bread with herring; she drinks some water, continues to read, and without having laughed once, she announces to the servants that she's going to bed.

Since she's not used to napping during the day, she tosses and turns in her bed, formulating a plan: in the middle of the night, when the rest of the palace is sleeping, she'll go over to the other side and explore. No one will follow her around; no one will distract her. She gets out of bed and takes the key ring from her dressing table, setting it down next to her, determined to rest just for a moment, to clear her mind for her upcoming expedition. But she falls into a deep sleep. When she begins to dream, the key covered in leather, the one for the forbidden purple door, gets up, dragging the chain behind it, and fits itself between her legs. There it nestles against her and finds its path, traveling far past her thighs.

The Forest Girl feels this in her dream, and without meaning to, she begins to sway her hips as if she's walking. The key becomes one with her womanly body. The girl experiences an unfamiliar pleasure, one she's never felt before. She would have been unable to understand what was happening even if she had been awake. In her dream, she no longer walks, she's running, pumping her hips, the key does the rest of the work, giving her pleasure that's almost painful. But she doesn't wake up. She opens her legs. Without wanting to, without knowing what's happening, she gives herself to the key, drunk with pleasure.

She doesn't awaken until the following morning. She's astonished to find the key chain wrapped around her naked legs. Disgusted, she removes it from her body and jumps out of bed. She puts the keys in a drawer. She promises herself to never enter the rooms of the Illuminata, the Lady of Light, ever again.

Promises, promises, promises. The morning has yet to end when she takes the key chain from its hiding place and turns the first key in its lock. No sooner does she cross the threshold than she is offered cheese and bread, which, without her realizing it, return her to childhood. She explores the rooms and their treasures with even greater curiosity. A woman carries a tray—identical to the ones the footmen are passing—bearing the head of a handsome man. She realizes it's a reference to the Bible and thinks that must be the case with the naked youth in the painting, an Adam attempting to seduce God. In this context the man's head doesn't disgust her; it stirs her curiosity.

She recognizes more biblical allusions in some of the paintings, and in the tableaux presented by the servants—on the patio she sees Joseph at the well, surrounded by his brothers—but she can't identify other paintings, of epic battles she doesn't recognize and women on horseback.

In the second to last room there's an oil painting of an Alaskan landscape, the lands that the Russians recently sold to America. This canvas disturbs her more than any other. It's almost completely white. But every color has been captured in the various tones of its whiteness. The stretch of snow conveys something like words, perhaps something even more precise. The canvas seems to speak words in a way that changes the quality of the silence. She's afraid when she looks at this painting, afraid of this whole wing of the palace. It all scares her. She finds it hard to breathe.

She returns to the part of the palace she knows and shuts herself in her rooms.

She walks up and down a long hallway until she's calm. She's determined that this time she will not fall asleep and will return when there's no one supervising her. But the night is cold, and her bones begin to ache. She's alone; she's said goodnight to Maslova. The cold that comes on when the sun sets is harder to bear, it doesn't just seep through keyholes into your body, it's like a claw.

She loosens her clothing. She gets into bed, wrapping herself in the covers. She doesn't lie down; although her bones are begging her to, she remains seated. Forgetting what happened the previous night, she puts the key chain at her side, thinking that she'll get up without lighting the candle, so the light through her window doesn't alert people that she's leaving this part of the palace. She plans to leave her room under the cover of darkness.

The keys don't trouble her tonight. Is it because, after many years (decades) without turning the complicated mechanism of those locks, doing so has exhausted them? The previous day they had turned a lock twice. For the metal pins and tumblers of the second lock, the penetration of the key was a major event. When it felt the key's metal teeth, the lock's interior went wild, accustomed as it was to nothing more than a mild, gentle breath of air. For a fraction of a second, it wasn't sure whether to seize up at the intrusion, forsaking the purpose for which it had been created.

The first pin in the lock tried to resist the key. Groaning, it attempted to halt the invasion. But the second piece of the mechanism gave the command that awoke the others, reminding them why they were created, moving them not out of duty but out of pleasure: the key had made contact. Air is just air; it's not solid, but you can feel it, though the sensation is delicate. And words are to groans as the key is to the air that passes through the lock!

When the lock felt the teeth of the key, an overwhelming, carnal pleasure made the second pin of the mechanism give way, and the first could no longer resist when the third and the fourth—every pin in the cylinder—turned obediently, letting themselves go. The lock, which was still young, despite years of being untouched, extended its hands in joy, with promises and lively conversation for all three keys, because the other two felt the caress of the third through the key chain, and when the lock groaned with pleasure, they responded as if three were one, electrified. The effort, despite exhausting them, was extremely pleasurable—a vertiginous delight.

Lying in bed next to the Forest Girl, as they prepare to sleep, the keys admit to one another how satisfying it is to perform their function.

"How fortunate we are!"

"We can't complain!"

And this confession leaves them in peace, satisfied, sleeping the sleep of the blessed.

The Forest Girl awakens after midnight. The rest of the palace's inhabitants are still fast asleep, dreaming their first dreams of the night. She gets out of bed, holding the key chain in her right hand. She puts on her slippers, throws a shawl over her shoulders, and, with her left hand, grabs the little candle and matches she uses to read at night. When she leaves her room, she shuts the door and hides the candle as planned, to prevent anyone from seeing a light in her window. She heads toward the rooms of the Lady of Light.

The girl has never left her room at night. The palace looks completely different in the dark. The shadows, the sound of her footsteps, the arrangement of the objects as she passes them, everything terrifies her, but she masters her fear and forges ahead.

The first key easily opens the door to the other side of the palace, where night seems like day. The room is blazing with various points of white light, intense but not harsh or severe, a warm, steady light. The room seems larger. The light is coming from the objects inside it—the paintings, the chairs, the carpet—not from candles or lamps. The brightest light comes from the bottle next to the book with *Genie* in its title. Every spine, every title is legible: *The Broken Skull, The Animal Who Slept Like a Log, Onionskins, Heartless Poems, The Unfeeling Heart.* The books are arranged by color and size; there is neither rhyme nor reason to the jumble of titles. Each object is next to its corresponding book, so that the size of the globe determines where the book (*Treatise on Geography*) sits on the shelf.

She extinguishes the candle in one breath but keeps it in her hand. She approaches the bottle and, blinking in the intense light, which hurts her eyes, sees a tiny man gesticulating inside. It seems like he wants to speak to her; he's moving his lips and his body expressively. The little man in the bottle kneels, his hands pressed together, looking at her. He appears to be asking her to free him from the bottle; he's begging her.

The Forest Girl picks up the bottle. The little man jumps with joy. He looks her in the eyes. He's no longer trying to speak. He reaches out to her. The young woman removes the bottle's lid and the little man escapes through its glass neck, growing long and thin to fit and then expanding again when he's out. Once outside the bottle, he shakes himself and begins to grow, more and more and more. His body's size doubles each second, he becomes so tall he can no longer stand, he bends down and doubles over as he continues to grow. His body begins to bump into the walls, taking up all the space, pushing the furniture back and knocking over anything in his way—amphorae, clocks—until he's filled the whole room. The Forest Girl presses herself against the door through which she entered.

The Forest Girl watches the body of the man from the bottle expand toward her, right up to the doorframe where she has taken refuge. She opens the door and passes through it. The body of the man from the bottle continues to grow, pursuing her. She wants to shut the door behind her, pushing with all her might against the mass of the giant man. "Ow!" the man from the bottle says. "You're pinching me! You're hurting me!" His voice resonates, echoing off the walls, but the Forest Girl pays no heed to his cries, afraid that his enormity will cross over and invade the other wing of the palace.

"Get out of here!"

"You're hurting me. . . . You're pinching me! Don't do that! Owwww!"

The Forest Girl pushes with all her might and manages to close the door. She turns the lock, and, without removing the key (she leaves her hand on it for what seems like an eternity), she tries to hear what's happening on the other side of the door, wondering what to do.

A loud crash. Something has broken. Silence. The growth of the man, his expansion, must have been contained, or else things would still be breaking as they were pushed out of the way, she would hear it. She puts the palm of her hand on the door. Nothing. But she doesn't dare open the door to be sure. She takes the keys. She still holds the candle in one hand, but she's lost the matches. She doesn't know whether she dropped them on the other side of the door or over here. She feels around on the floor, but she can't find them. Her eyes are adjusting to the darkness, but she still can't see her surroundings clearly. She goes to her room, slowly and very carefully, so as not to bump into anything and cause a stir. She doesn't want to make noise and awaken the servants. Bit by bit, she feels her way along, taking each step with care, and finally she arrives. She paces back and forth, unsure of what to do. Eventually she calms down. She goes to bed, though it takes her a long time to fall asleep.

She dreams that a priest is sleeping. A woman approaches him to cut off his beard and his long hair. She dreams what the priest is dreaming: that a pack of hounds is attacking the giant man. That someone is watching this scene and doing nothing, despite the fact that he holds the dogs' leashes in his hand. That in the pools of blood pouring forth from the giant, there are flocks of birds. Things keep happening to the dream giant, but the Forest Girl becomes distracted by the dreamer, examining the dress of this handsome bearded man. He awakens and says, "When I saw the giant, I saw my country, my beloved country, and its people."

Then she dreams she's the one inside the bottle, a bottle on the shelf of a bookcase. No one comes to let her out. In her dream, she wonders if she would become a giant too if she were set free. And she notices her bottle doesn't have a mouth.

She awakens late the following morning.

She calls Maslova. While the girl is helping her, she asks whether there's been any commotion on the other side.

"Commotion? On the other side? Of what?"

"I thought I heard something during the night on the other side of the palace. . . . A . . . a commotion. . . ."

"Nope! No commotion! What a notion! Silence, just like always. We received madame's correspondence, though, as usual. And sent over the cheeses that arrived early in the morning, the ones ordered for you. The only strange thing was that they asked whether some matches belonged to us, you've never seen such long matches, twice as long as your arm. Three long matches . . . we took them to the kitchen. They're really quite a sight."

The Forest Girl doesn't hear this story about the matches; she's overwhelmed by images from her dream.

"Some dogs . . ." She can still hear the barking of the hound dogs.

"Dogs?"

"I dreamed that someone was dreaming about them."

The Forest Girl cannot get the giant from the bottle or the sleeping bearded man out of her head; to master her thoughts, she says, "Last night I dreamed one dream after another." Her craving for the cheeses is the only thing that draws her to the door to the other side.

The first lock opens as it always has before; the key turns easily inside the keyhole of the door that leads to the other side of the palace. The bottle is in its place. It's not empty, but in the shadows of the bookcase, it's impossible to tell what's inside it. Whatever it is, it's not moving, it's not emitting any light at all, and it certainly doesn't look like a small person. The room is in perfect order; nothing seems to be damaged or broken.

That day she tries the second key. The lock turns easily. Four huge frescoes cover the walls from floor to ceiling, each one filled with dozens of people, and each one with a peculiar characteristic: some of the objects in them are three-dimensional, jutting out from the wall into the room—tables, lamps, the clothes people are wearing. There's even a faun's tail sticking out of one painting, hard, as if it's made of plaster, sprouting from the wall. The ceiling, which is painted like the sky—blue, luminous, with thin, wispy clouds—looks like a falling roof around the edges, with loose bricks trailing ivy.

Her skirt grazes a skirt in one of the paintings. The person she brushes against is wearing the exact same skirt that she herself is wearing. She begins to feel uneasy. She retraces her steps, passing through the library without stopping, and the grand hall as well, locking the door behind her. She spends the rest of the day in her rooms with a sense of foreboding.

The following morning she feels confident again. She uses the first and the second keys, passing through both doors, and without hesitation, she even turns the third key in its lock. Unlike the others, it makes a scraping sound and squeaks like rusty metal, despite the fact that it's covered in leather. She remembers the admonition but disregards it.

She passes through the forbidden door, which is purple on the inside as well.

The room is not a room, it's a forest—the cold, dark forest of her childhood. She recognizes a path. She walks, the cold burning her feet and hands. The sun rises in a gray sky, warming the earth. Birds sing. Everything is familiar. She proceeds without hesitation. She comes to her parents' cottage. She opens the door. A woman and her two lovely daughters are sitting at a table with her father. She recognizes him instantly. He looks at her coldly, examining her.

"It's me, Father." She looks him in the eyes and remembers her name, as if it's written on the woodsman's pupils. "I'm Anna. Where is Mother?"

"I used to have a daughter. She didn't look anything like you."

"It's me. You gave me to the Illuminata. Who are these people?"

"This woman is my wife. And these are her daughters, the only ones I have. Your mother died years ago."

"You have three daughters, Father. Where did you bury Mother?"

Her father gives her some vague directions rather brusquely. The Forest Girl, Anna, goes alone to visit her grave. A chunk of stone surrounded by weeds marks her burial place.

"If only this poor stone were clean. . . ."

Anna gets to work. She pulls up the weeds and cleans what she can, decorating the stone with what flowers she finds, washing it over and over again, making it more beautiful than anyone could have foreseen. Her stepmother and her sisters watch her working hard, covering their mouths so she can make out only their snide laughter.

She returns home. The woman says, "You certainly like to clean, eh? Why don't you clean my kitchen. . . ."

The Forest Girl cleans the pots and mops the floor.

When they've finished eating—though they don't offer her any food—she tries to return to the Illuminata's rooms. All she wants is to pass through them and return to her bed to sleep; she's so tired, she's not even hungry. But there's no keyhole for the key. The purple door is sealed tightly shut.

The night is cold. She returns to her father's house and lies down to sleep in the ashes by the hearth.

Alone with her husband, the woman asks, "Is she really your daughter?"

"Yes, without a doubt. She's the one I gave to the Illuminata."

"I always thought that was an old wives' tale. If she's your daughter, she'll have to live with us. She can help me in the kitchen. I could use it."

The next morning, Anna cleans the chicken coop, collects apples, prepares the soup, makes the bread, and separates the lentils.

The household no longer suffers from hunger or scarcity. The woodsman has had a stroke of luck. One day when he chopped down a tree, he discovered hidden treasure—gold ingots, emeralds—and became a rich man. He built more rooms for the cottage. His wife and her two daughters began to dress well. But they didn't allow Anna to set foot in the new rooms. "You—stay there! You belong in the kitchen."

One day when her father is going to the fair he asks her, "What would you like me to bring back for you? Your sisters have asked for dresses and necklaces."

"I'd like a branch of peach blossoms, my mother's favorite."

When the woodsman returns from the fair (where it's likely he did some naughty things; ever since he came into money he's let himself go), the Forest Girl takes the branch of peach blossoms to her mother's grave. The stepmother tells her daughters, "Stupid girl, she has a chance to dress like a lady, and instead she asks for a sentimental nothing!"

After that they pay her no attention.

Anna sits down next to the peach blossom branch and begins to sing. Then she cries. We can all agree this is sentimental behavior. But it reflects Anna's frame of mind: she is exhausted from spending her days cleaning, bewildered to find herself the protagonist of two different stories, filled with regret for forgetting her parents and disobeying the Illuminata. All this, combined with her age (being young doesn't help much), makes her feel like Cinderella. We can also agree that thinking of herself as Cinderella is slightly corny. But it doesn't seem corny to her at all. Anna has become the Forest Girl, and the Forest Girl has become Cinderella.

What happens next is, the peach blossom branch soaks up her tears. Considering the state the branch is in, and its flowers and its fruit and its environment, her tears are like mother's milk. This is not a recommendation to the reader, and even less of a magic formula, because wine is better than tears, better than knowledge, and far better than any story, and champagne is better than wine, and opium is better than any alcohol. But this is dangerous logic, because the type of bird and birdsong each of these causes requires careful consideration.

Every day, when she finishes working, Anna visits her mother's grave and the branch of peach blossoms and sheds tears. And the branch begins to grow into a peach tree. And a variety of brambles and blackberries springs up around her feet. Anna weaves the brambles around the stone and the tree. When Anna cries, she dances; blame it on the birds, the nightingales, the owls.

The birds sing and nest in the tree. The woodsman has no knack for growing things. He likes chopping things down. By the time he discovered his stash of gold and precious stones, he'd done a lot of chopping, and all around his home there was nothing but bare earth, which the rain and the snow eroded. His axe dreams it has been mistreated. There are landslides every day. That's why the birds take refuge in the peach tree. With nothing like it for miles around, it's like the capital of Eden. And they would do anything Anna asks, because the woodsman's daughter has given them their only shelter.

The birds protect her. She is hungry no longer. She is cold no longer. But she continues to sleep in the ashes in the kitchen, and the three women continue to mistreat her while her father pays her no heed. Her face is always dirty, like her clothes.

One day, there is a proclamation from the king: all the young women in the kingdom are invited to a ball. The king is seeking a wife for his son. He's tired of him being a bachelor, tired of him rejecting all the candidates he proposes, tired of him carousing like a madman; the king wants him to settle down. And he wants a grandson, to secure the future of his crown. If he leaves the prince to his devices, the crown will pass out of the family.

"What, there's not a single woman who lives up to your expectations?" he harangues his son each morning. And at lunchtime, "I offer you the hand of an emperor's daughter, and you reject her. What's wrong with you? Why is no one good enough for you?" In the evenings, the tone of the king's discourse is more elevated. "Do you want something better than reality?"

"Let's start with your choice of words, Father. Can you call a young lady 'something'? They're people!"

When Anna's stepsisters hear the proclamation, they begin preparing their outfits, overjoyed. Anna asks permission to go.

She's not thinking of the prince, and far less of finding a husband. She just wants to dance.

"Absolutely not. How dare you even ask? You should have asked your father to bring you a dress from the fair! But you missed that opportunity. What will you wear? We'd be ashamed to be seen with you," her stepmother shoots back spitefully.

"Please, ma'am. . . ."

"Out of the question. And call me *mother*! How impertinent, calling me *ma'am*!"

On the day of the ball, Anna asks permission to go once more, when the foursome—father, stepmother, and her two daughters—are dressed to the nines, ready to go. The women regard her with cold, mocking eyes. Her stepmother picks up the pot with the lentils Anna has cleaned and dumps it in the ashes of the fireplace. She says, "If you can clean the lentils in half an hour, you can go. But don't come anywhere near us if you do. . . ."

The foursome depart without looking back; they don't give her a second thought. Anna watches them out of the corner of her eye. They look hideous. Her father's suit is shiny. "How embarrassing, he looks like some low-class government functionary!" The young ladies are dressed in painfully bad taste.

Anna calls to the birds in the peach tree, singing:

> Live blossoms of the peach tree in bloom,
> Sort the good from the bad.
> I want to dance and be loved.

A dozen different birds fly into the kitchen, fishing the lentils out of the fireplace, leaving them clean in the bowl. Anna goes to the peach tree and asks:

> Father of live flowers,
> Help me to dress beautifully.
> I want to dance and be loved.

A dozen new birds bring her a gold dress and a pair of golden slippers, laying them on the clean kitchen table.

Anna bathes (in cold water—all birds hate hot water), does her hair, and dresses. The slippers make her feel lighter; she usually wears a pair of rough wooden clogs. In these slippers she runs—practically flies—to the king's castle, and she doesn't slow down when she arrives. She's lighter and more agile than all the matrons and spoiled girls in the room—overfed and pudgy—who are trying to catch the prince's eye. In comparison, Anna looks like a pixie.

The prince sees her and tells the king:

> Father of mine, amongst these live blossoms
> I can sort the good from the bad.
> She's the one.
> I want to dance and be loved.

The king doesn't think much of her. She doesn't move with "dignity," but neither does she move like a peasant. What is she? Beautiful, yes, and she seems to have good manners. He holds his son's arm until she begins to move her arms and feet more gracefully than he has ever beheld. Then he releases the prince, who shoots off like a bullet—a clumsy expression, but there's no better way to describe it.

The prince dances with Anna all night. They're like two figures in a music box. Magnetic, almost mechanical. When some aristocrat or other approaches him between songs to introduce his daughter, the prince, instead of replying, "With pleasure," repeats:

> I have chosen amongst these living blossoms
> To love and be loved.

And the aristocrats think to themselves, *What a foolish young man, how can he not see how lovely my daughter is!* But their daughters aren't lovely. They look like pom-poms, or perhaps muffs made from fine furs.

When the clock strikes midnight, two dozen colorful little birds enter the palace; "tweet tweet tweet," they say sharply. No one has ever seen such a cloud of birds at this hour in these parts. The birds take Anna's dress by the waist and lift her. It's quite a sight to see: Anna rising, her golden dress floating around her. Far away some little bird sings (and fortunately almost no one hears it, but the prince does, though he doesn't understand):

Oh, your perfume!
Pretty Anna-bella!
Oh, your perfume, your perfume!
The scent of your lovely legs!

No one delights in this scene more than the prince. Unsurprised, unafraid, he thinks it's a new dance step and is filled with a rare joy. Which is why, when Anna disappears from sight (a speedy ascension), he is the first to notice that one of her golden slippers remains on the floor. It is small and smells like peaches. The rest of the crowd stands staring at the sky, wondering what has just happened; the prince picks up the dainty slipper and puts it in his pocket.

The prince's suit has large, well-made pockets; they aren't just for decoration. He uses them to carry small bottles of ointment that keeps babies away.

The next morning, the prince, full of vigor for lack of having spent the night in his usual amorous pursuits, goes from house to house with the slipper in his hands, searching for the young woman who has bewitched him. When he arrives at the home of the rich man who was once a woodsman, the eldest daughter tries the slipper on in her room. Her big toe is too long.

"Don't worry," her mother says. "Cut it off. What will it matter if you have a limp once you're queen. Anna!" she shouts up the service stairs.

"Yes, ma'am!"

"Will you stop calling me ma'am! Lower your voice. Quick, bring your father's axe, you lazy girl, hurry!"

The stepmother's daughter chops off her toe. She puts the slipper on and suffers in silence.

The prince follows her into his handsome copper-leaf carriage with its painted roof. When they pass the peach tree, the birds sing:

> You've got yourself a trimmed hoof,
> You saw the good but chose the bad.

The prince looks at the pretty young lady's foot. The dainty golden slipper is soaked in blood. He knocks on the roof of the carriage and gives an order to return to the woodsman's house.

"You tricked me. You offered me an unblemished foot and gave me a mutilated one. I don't want this girl. You'll pay the price!"

Anna's stepmother and the woodsman betray the girl, pretending not to know what she has done, saying, among other things, "Devil child! How could you do such a thing to the prince! Go to your room without dinner!" and begging the prince's pardon. The stepmother orders Anna to clean the slipper. When it's clean the stepmother gives it to her second daughter.

"Run! Go try it on, now! And it better fit, because if it doesn't the prince will have all our heads!"

Again she shouts up the service stairs, "Aaaannaaa! Quick, take your father's axe upstairs, hurry, hurry!"

The girl, who isn't remotely pretty, tries on the slipper, but her heel doesn't fit. She doesn't say a word to her mother: she chops off her heel in one swing and puts the slipper on. Swallowing the pain, she goes downstairs and smiles at the prince, as if she's been dancing with him all night.

The prince has a pure heart and believes her.

It's important to explain that his heart is pure. It is part of the reason why his father wants to marry him off. The prince is quick to trust, but not stupid, and just as quick to distrust, which doesn't make for a good ruler. Power isn't built on innocence or candidness, and his father is right, this prince wouldn't amount to much of a king. His search for a good wife has as much to do with perpetuating his dynasty as with building alliances.

The prince, excited and giddy with love, invites the woodsman's wife's second daughter into his princely carriage. When they are halfway to the palace, birds of all sizes from the peach tree surround them, singing:

Of all the good things you had to choose
You chose the worst of all.
You've got yourself a trimmed hoof.
She's not the one, she's not the one.

The idea of looking at his beloved slipper and finding it soaked in blood again turns the prince's stomach. Which is why we must digress once more. We can't just pass by a prince's upset stomach. Much has been written about empty bellies—not that it's made much difference. But can the same be said for the upset stomachs of pure-hearted princes? Let's make a few distinctions: it's one thing to overeat, and another to have had enough of human blood, and another altogether not to be able to look at something because you're too sensitive. The last was the case with the prince.

He has only to look into her eyes to see that the birds are singing the truth. He doesn't look down. He stares at her hypocritical face, her eyes like empty spoons, shining at the thought of her title, her father-in-law, the throne. Two eyes that, the prince realizes, are blind to him. They don't look at him the way they looked at him the previous night.

The carriage returns to the woodsman's cottage. They ask the young lady to be so kind as to get out. She leaves dark, nearly black footprints on the stone floors. The birds from the peach tree surround the carriage, singing:

There are unscathed feet in this house.
Here's the one that wears gold,
Her foot as lovely as her soul.

For some unexplained reason this verse is accompanied by music. Where are the guitars, harps, and lutes? But this is no time for the prince to worry about such things. He gets out of the carriage, avoiding the bloody footprints, and crosses the woodsman's threshold again.

The family of four looks at him in horror. Not realizing the prince is there, Anna enters the room, her hands still wet from washing the slipper once more, singing, "Here you are, I've washed it for you again, the gold fabric is so fine, it's easy to clean."

Everyone turns to look at her. Anna sees the prince. He recognizes her eyes. Anna puts on the slipper. The cloud of birds enters the house, draping the golden dress over her. The prince's footman brings her the other slipper, which they have put in his hands, and the birds arrange Anna's hair.

That night, once again, she and the prince dance, but not like the previous night, because Anna begins to feel pressured. At midnight she remembers the Illuminata, certain that she's going to come for her. She's filled with regret, then fear. And her fear grows throughout the night. Although she no longer sleeps in the ashes, but in the room her mother slept in, it makes no difference. Her fear continues to grow. She thinks her mother will come too. That the birds have betrayed her. That they'll attack her body. But she doesn't have the body of a giant, and no dogs will spring forth from her blood to protect her. She has no choice. She must confront the Illuminata before returning for her prince.

At the first light of day she walks into the forest to find the path to the Illuminata's palace. There's a tiny hole in the purple door. She pokes at the hole with a stick. Both her hands become covered in fine gold dust. The hole turns into a lock; Anna slides the key in and opens the door.

The Forest Girl shuts the door, locking it behind her, and runs to wash her hands. No matter how she soaps, scrubs, and rinses her fingers, she can't get rid of the gold color. Her face has changed, too: the brightness of the room and the fact that she now knows there's something on the other side of the purple door fill her heart with deep regret. She wants to go back and dance with the prince despite the fact that if she does, everything will turn to gold, just like it did for Midas.

That same afternoon, the Illuminata returns to the palace. She notices the girl's face has changed.

"Did you open the door I told you not to?"

The Forest Girl says she didn't. ("No, ma'am, I don't know how to lie.")

"Are you certain you didn't turn the lock I specifically told you not to?"

The Forest Girl shakes her head again.

The Illuminata asks a third time, and once more the Forest Girl lies to her, denying it vehemently. The Illuminata sees her golden fingers.

"You're lying!"

The Forest Girl falls into a deep slumber, and when she awakens, she's back in the forest. She would scream, but she's lost her voice. She looks for a path, some way out, back to the Illuminata's palace, or the prince's, or the woodsman's cottage, but the forest seems endless. Her feet sink into the mud. She loses her slippers.

A few days pass; her clothes and her body are no longer what they were when she lived in luxury, wanting for nothing. Her hair is tangled. Her stockings are loose. She has given up trying to find a way out. She eats herbs, berries, mushrooms, and roots. Sitting against the trunk of a large tree, she feels the desire to sing, but no sound comes out of her mouth.

Twelve horses pass by, carrying eleven knights and their king. The Forest Girl doesn't get up; she thinks she's dreaming. The king falls in love with her at first sight; he's never seen anyone so beautiful. He asks her name but she can't answer.

"Who are you? Where are you from? What are you doing here?"

The Forest Girl can't say a single word. The fact that she's mute makes the king like her even more. *Silence is golden.* The Forest Girl shows him her golden finger. It doesn't bother the king, so he takes her with him. When he returns to his kingdom, he announces that he's going to marry her. The queen mother and his sisters try to dissuade him, but the king stands firm.

Once again, the Forest Girl eats and dresses well; she soon forgets what she has done and that she's been evicted from paradise. The gold on her finger doesn't disappear. At night, when she sleeps, the golden finger does what the leather-bound key once did. It nestles between her legs and finds a way to give her pleasure.

The wedding takes place, the Forest Girl shares her bed with the king before he retires to his rooms, and after several encounters, she is surprised to discover how pleasurable it is to be with him in this way. The king loves her. The Forest Girl loves the pleasure she gives the king, loves his velvet and his satin, loves how well the servants treat her. She loves her hairdresser, who ornaments her hair with precious stones. She loves the baker, who makes delicious pastries. She loves the kingdom's cheeses and its bread. She also loves her memory of a ball that lasted all night in a gorgeous palace. And even more than that ball, she loves the gaze and the arms of her prince.

• • •

One night when she's falling asleep, she sees her whole life, from when she had a father, a mother, hunger, and a name (Anna) to when she became the Forest Girl. Then she went back to being Anna, but her name was Cinderella, and then she became a queen. How does one girl become another, and then another? Her story is one of hunger and laughter, then one of adoption by a cold, luminous woman who gives her the keys to know herself and tests her. And before she even learns what she likes, the keys take advantage of her, making her feel a pleasure she neither understands nor wants, playing—without her realizing it—with what she ought to have been seeking. Sleep takes its hold, and she has a dream in which she becomes the Girl Who Walked on Bread:

Once upon a time there was a woodsman who lived with his wife at the edge of a poor village. They lived in misery; in front of their hut, there was a muddy stream swarming with flies. Because the woodsman and his wife were devout, peaceful people who were more virtuous than any of their neighbors, the saints blessed them with a strikingly beautiful daughter. Though she was lovely to behold, she was arrogant and mean-hearted. She looked down on her parents for their poverty and gentleness. She called them shameful names. She liked to step on her mother's apron for fun.

"What are we going to do with her?" her mother would say. "She has every reason to look down on us: we're poor, we're humble, but she's all we have! Today she steps on my apron, tomorrow she'll step on my face."

The girl played with the flies by the muddy stream, plucking off their wings and delighting in their suffering. She speared the largest ones with her mother's sewing needle, pinning them to the pages of a book, saying, "This one knows how to read." When her mother tried to teach her the alphabet, she refused. "Reading is for flies."

The girl grew quickly, as did her wickedness and the poverty that surrounded her. She tortured the two chickens in the coop to death and hid their bodies to keep anyone from eating them. Famine and plague descended on the village. The girl was hungry every day; her stomach seemed to be eating itself. The girl's parents sent her away with an acquaintance who worked in the count's castle. No sooner had the count and countess set eyes on her—so proud and good-looking—than they took her into their service. They dressed her in satin and silk, in beautiful dresses and shoes. They had her hair done. She looked like a young lady; she ran errands for the women of the court and charmed arriving guests. The count was especially fond of her. He was a man of the flesh, and he could hardly wait for her to come of age so he could take her as a lover. He flattered her and lavished her with gifts, laying the groundwork for his plan. "There's no one more beautiful than you," he would say, complimenting her at every opportunity, because he had yet to possess her. He said this over and over and was quite compelling. The count wasn't interested in girls, but her body was becoming more and more like a woman's.

The countess, who wanted nothing more than to please her husband—particularly when there was some benefit to her—pretended to think highly of the girl too. She took particular care in dressing the girl, spoiling her. *What will happen one day when my husband doesn't want her anymore, where will we send her? And what if she bears him a child? I don't want to have it here, we'll send it to her parents, who'll look after it as if it were their own.* And thinking such thoughts, she sent the girl to visit her parents.

The young woman put on her finest clothes. She wanted everyone in her "dumpy village" to envy her, wanted to humiliate them with her elegance. When the count's carriage left her at the entrance to her village, which was so small and poor that its streets were too narrow for the carriage, she saw some children playing beside the well, and her mother, who was carrying a bundle of firewood on her back and some root vegetables for dinner in her hands. The girl felt so ashamed to have such a "dirty" "nothing" of a mother that she turned around and walked off with all her gifts, getting back into the carriage.

"Miss?" the driver asked, so taken aback he was unable to speak further.

"You keep these gifts, sir, and don't tell anyone, just take me back to the palace . . . but let's take our time so no one becomes suspicious. . . ."

They stopped at a roadside inn and had a few drinks, speaking of unladylike things. Such a precocious girl! The driver began to sing, and the girl teased him.

A few months later, the countess, still worried, decided to send the girl to visit her parents again. She said, "Poor thing! So far from your family, don't you miss them? I've got a magnificent Italian-style loaf of bread for you to take them. And a basket of cheeses, too—but I didn't include oysters, I thought they wouldn't survive the trip, and we don't want to poison your parents, we want to honor them, don't we?"

The girl just wanted to poison them. But to stay in the good graces of the countess, whom she was eager to please, she dressed in her finest clothes, took the gifts, and got into the carriage.

On the way there, the skies opened up, but the driver kept going, then the rain stopped, and the sun came out. The sky was shining brightly when he left the girl at the entrance to her village.

Cursing her luck, she got out of the carriage with her gifts. She lifted her skirts to keep them out of the mud. The narrow streets were empty; everyone had gone inside for shelter from the rain. The muddy stream in front of her parents' house had swollen with the rains, the stones for crossing it submerged deep underwater. To keep her shoes clean, she put the bread on the ground and stepped on it. The bread sank into the mud under her weight, and an eddy pulled her into the stream. She was caught in a whirlpool and was soon submerged and pulled to the bottom.

On the muddy riverbed, a witch was brewing beer. The smell coming from the kegs was revolting. Clouds of flies danced next to spiders. The young woman hugged her loaf of bread, wondering, *Did I do something wrong, trying to keep my shoes clean?*

Time passed. Beneath the water, the young woman could hear what her mother and father were saying about her, and the other people in the village too. They despised her arrogance, they thought she was stupid, and no one mentioned her beauty. "How stupid can you be, thinking that a loaf of bread will keep you afloat?!"

The girl who stepped on the loaf of bread was the laughing stock of the village. In his castle, the count found another lover whose downfall the countess is already plotting.

The queen awakens from her dream about the girl with the bread, certain that no one remembers who she is. A few days later, she gives birth to a boy. The Illuminata attends the baptism. When the Forest Girl is getting ready for bed, before her golden finger traces its usual path between the sheets and her thighs, the Illuminata appears.

"Did you open the door I forbade you to open?"

The Illuminata shines just as brightly as the forbidden room. The queen shakes her head.

"Think carefully about how you answer me. What will it cost you to tell the truth? If you lie, you'll lose your son. Don't you love your son? Answer me truthfully: did you open the door I forbade you to?"

The queen shakes her head.

The Illuminata disappears, taking the boy with her.

The queen mother and the other ladies of the court think the queen has eaten her own child. They tell the king he should punish his wife by exiling her from his kingdom. But the king loves her and refuses to believe she's a cannibal. The queen writes him a long letter telling him everything. The Illuminata makes the ink disappear and all the king sees is a blank sheet of paper. The queen writes to him again, but to the king her words appear to be written in water.

The couple is blessed with another child, a girl. The queen postpones the baptism, afraid the same thing will happen again. But the baptism is celebrated before the end of the year, according to the custom of the country. The Illuminata is in the crowd. Before the queen comes out onto the balcony, the Illuminata appears to her in the royal chambers and asks, "Do you love your daughter?"

The queen nods silently.

"Tell me the truth. Did you open that room in the palace?"

Once again, the Forest Girl denies it. The Illuminata picks up the little girl and vanishes.

This time even the king cannot protect his wife. The queen is taken to the gallows. She climbs the steps with bare feet. She's been stripped of her finery.

The Illuminata appears like a shadow at the top of the steps leading to her death.

"Did you open the lock?" she asks. "Save your life, confess!"

The queen raises her golden index finger and nods yes. Before the crowd, the Illuminata makes the king's children appear, one in each of the queen's arms. They don't put the noose around her neck. They put the royal cloak around her shoulders as she holds her children.

All three executioners spend the afternoon trying to put the noose around the Illuminata's neck. But each time they think they've succeeded, her head is somewhere else. Two of them end up hanging each other. Only one remains. Obeying the light emitted by this frozen woman, the last executioner puts the noose around his own neck and hangs himself.

When night falls, the queen goes to the window. Her children are sleeping. The king is attending to his duties. The queen mother is plotting; rumors are flying in the court. The Illuminata passes in front of the royal palace followed by the youth of the city, celebrating with pipes and drums. Some dance, others turn somersaults, some stamp their feet and sing. They're drunk with joy.

Because she's alone, Anna, the Forest Girl, Cinderella, the queen, tries to speak. At first, all that comes out is a rasping sound, but then her throat clears, and a stream of words tumbles forth—everything you have just read.

PART FIVE

FINALE

♛

St. Petersburg, June 1905

39. After Reading

Claudia finishes the last line of Anna's manuscript. "That's it?" She's not satisfied by the ending. She flips through the other version of the novel to see if it had a different one in its previous incarnation. "What? This other manuscript is completely different! No girl, no Illuminata, no queen, no king, no stepmother, no witches, no fairies. It's a completely different story about Peter the Great's African, Gannibal, an adventure. I'll read it tomorrow."

The sun has yet to rise. Claudia has a long, difficult day ahead. She carefully returns the second manuscript to its box. When she's about to set the bound manuscript on top of it, a loose page slips out.

It's a different kind of paper entirely, pale pink, a faint trace of scent remains: "A perfumed letter." It's covered from top to bottom in handwriting even smaller than the second manuscript's, tight calligraphy traced carefully by Karenina. Like the words have been painted. At the top, it says, "Strictly private. For A.V."

"It's a love letter!" Claudia's heart skips a beat. She's thrilled; she adores a love story. "A.V.? It's for Vronsky! What does it say?" Claudia reads it aloud quietly, in her own sweet voice. "My love: what I have experienced with you is shameful, but I'm addicted."

She stops reading. Without realizing what she's doing, she has pressed the note against her breast. She's deeply moved. She sniffs the paper again.

"What could she be referring to? Is she replying to the note Vronsky wrote on the folded calling card? Is she talking about opium?"

Claudia is terribly excited—secrets thrill her even more than love stories. She's strung-out because she hasn't slept a wink, but she must read on to find out what she wants to know.

"Will she mention the opium? That must be what she's talking about!"

She summons the energy to begin reading aloud in a low voice:

"The first time I got to know you, in the biblical sense, I was pained and ashamed of myself. Not just because I had committed adultery; I have always found the conjugal act unpleasant. I never wanted to with my son's father. I was simply fulfilling my duty to him; I closed my eyes, and it was over soon enough, like most other bodily functions. It was like sweating beneath a heavy coat. But with you ... with you I kept my eyes open. That first time, my desire lay dormant. But in the encounters that followed, I discovered with you, and thanks to you, something I did not know existed: pleasure, the pleasure of two bodies in love. You opened a window inside me that I didn't even know was there.

"I want to tell you about that window. Unlike the rest of this edifice, instead of opening to the outside, it opened onto myself. Without the window your touch made me aware of—which you taught me to access myself—that window that sees with touch (not with sight) (though you say sight gives you pleasure, I have experienced my greatest ecstasy with my eyes shut, especially at night when there's no one around, no light), I would never have known a whole continent within myself. It's not that I'm someone different: the difference is that now I know my own borders. I understand my own body, that my borders extend beyond my own skin, far beyond myself. Getting to know myself is like crossing vast territories that ..."

The tight script ends in a broken sentence, as does Claudia's understanding. *This should never be mentioned*, she thinks in silence. *Is this what* The Book of Anna *is about too? I don't know. . . . But this isn't part of Tolstoy's novel, she disobeyed him, just like we have. I wonder if Tolstoy knew? Is that what the book I just read was about?*

Claudia is too tired to think clearly. It's rare that she doesn't get a good night's sleep. It's still pitch-black outside, but there's movement in the street. Her servants are sweeping the street in front of the house; there are so many pedestrians on Nevsky Prospekt that the rubbish must be cleared from the front of the house every day.

She puts Anna's note inside the bound manuscript, which she sets in the box covered with blue cloth, saying, "I'll read the first book another day, that's the one that Vorkuyev, the writer and publisher, thought was really good, the one that's a moral lesson. It can't be anything like this one. At all." She closes the box and ties the bow, trying to leave the knot and the creases in the ribbon the way she found them. She puts Vronsky's calling card back where she found it. She lights the little lamp she brought down from her bedroom and blows out the ones in the study.

She climbs the stairs to the bedrooms much more slowly than usual. Exhausted but aroused (*I'm like some crazy old goat*), she goes to Sergei's room instead of her own (*I'm certainly not going to sleep alone*), where he's sleeping soundly, smiling, his messy hair curly, not unlike the little boy he used to be, the one Anna adored. Claudia removes her slippers, extinguishes the little lamp, and gets in bed next to Sergei, embracing him. Sergei turns, but he doesn't notice her and keeps on sleeping. Claudia rolls over, and before she realizes it, she's asleep.

The first thing Claudia encounters in her dreams is a scene with three women, identical to a carefully posed photograph of the Countess Tolstaya: Sonya (or Sophia), Tolstoy's wife (she's one of the three models) feigns spontaneity sitting next to her daughter, with whom she's just had a bitter argument, and her niece, a born troublemaker, all three forcing smiles and pretending to be sweet, cozy, intimate.

In her dream, as in the photograph, light comes through a window, a harsh light that demands attention, much like the disguised mood of the sitters, who turn away from the corrosive ray and don't allow it to alter the sweetness Tolstaya is determined to project.

What is this image doing in Claudia's dream? But Claudia doesn't ask herself that; she asks, *Why am I not always here? This is where I belong, this is where I came from, I want to be with women.* And without saying another word, she joins the three women. She becomes frozen like them, but as in Sonya's photograph, she can feel movement; everything there looks dynamic, cozy, intimate, kind: like an inviting home, with its innate frenzy, its domestic energy, the sweet struggle to maintain order.

Some might specify that now they're four women, but Claudia doesn't need to be counted. She just wants to be with them, to be part of their world; it feels so natural to her to join in that gentle atmosphere the three Tolstayas are affecting.

In Claudia's dream, the three women are reflected in a mirror, which is being held by a princess who is imprisoned in the palace of the magician Koschei the Immortal. The princess spends two days pining away for the man she loves.

Then the women's faces merge into one, Claudia's. The Immortal looks into his magic mirror and sees the same thing as his prisoner, recognizing his daughter in Claudia's face.

"My daughter, Claudia, what's she doing in our mirror?"

Sergei appears in the reflection, alongside Claudia. The imprisoned princess (Claudia) looks into her mirror, too, and says, "It's the one I love, with someone else," and begins to cry. In the reflection, Sergei kisses Claudia (the daughter of the undying one).

The Immortal is afraid, because his death is imprisoned in his daughter Claudia's tears. What a man the Immortal is, keeping two prisoners: death and the princess. In this story, Claudia doesn't recognize the echoes of Rimsky-Korsakov's opera, the one she saw at the theater. At the sound of Rimsky-Korsakov's music, her dreams fall apart, fragmenting into several others that she won't remember come morning.

40. The Plot

Clementine is plotting. Together with her beloved Vladimir. The pain of his loss has altered him beyond recognition; he's become a lapdog, and more recently a rabid wolf. He's lost all sense of direction—a lapdog trailing after its owner, a wolf driven by rage.

Like Vladimir's two phases, the hunt for the dissidents is also submissive and raging, driven by desire for the tsar's approval, attacking the dissidents nonstop. Night and day, it doesn't cease. It's decimated the cell of Clementine's accomplices: most of them are dead or in prison, with the exception of Clementine, the only one who still roams the streets.

Vladimir has been busy, and not because Gapon has been sending him on missions. The reverend has gone from living in secret to living in exile—with Gorky, then Lenin, then Kropotkin. He no longer uses his talent for picking locks either.

Clementine and Vladimir want to do something extreme that will cause the downfall of the state "in all its forms." A contact gives them a valuable tip: Prince Orlov's automobile, which the tsar likes to use, will be driving down the Nevsky Prospekt on a certain date before noon. Why won't it be escorted by security forces? Because it will be a special trip to collect something very precious. "Could it possibly be a woman?" The tsar's not the type to risk his hide for a pair of legs. Fearful of assassination—he has been for years—he's sharp enough to realize this is a critical moment. Everything hangs in the balance—the present, the future, and the legacy of the past.

Because it's the automobile the tsar frequently uses, Clementine and Vladimir want to believe the tsar will be traveling inside. It's well worth their while to concoct a plan, the perfect opportunity for them to plant a bomb. Vladimir is inspired first: Clementine will cross Nevsky Prospekt precisely at the moment the automobile carrying the tsar is passing, forcing it to halt.

"If it doesn't slow down, run for your life, the plan won't work."

"I don't understand how those creatures work, the ones that consume kerosene and fascinate the enemies of the people."

"They're just like a horse and carriage, just faster and quite a bit noisier."

"I know how a horse moves, not these things."

"Watch them. Starting today, pay attention to their speed and how they run. That's the first thing, then . . ."

The two of them get more and more excited as they formulate their plan: "When you see the automobile coming, cross Nevsky with your back to the car. They'll slow down, and I'll cross the street behind them and put our bomb on the rear bumper."

"At least the wonderful invention of the bumper is good for something!"

"But how will we fasten it there?"

"It'll fall off!"

"Let's put it inside a cushion!"

"A cushion?"

"Yes, a nice plump cushion, that way it will fit wherever we put it, and we'll stuff it with explosives." The idea of putting a bomb inside a cushion would occur only to a seamstress. "A well-made, pretty pillow that looks like a gift for the tsar."

"Embroidered with the words 'Our Father.'"

"We'll light the fuse, which we'll run through a buttonhole, before we plant it."

"How will you keep the fuse from blowing out when it reaches the cushion?"

"It won't blow out, the cushion will catch fire, it will feed the flames."

"The automobile will start moving again, the bomb will explode a few seconds later, and farewell tyrant!"

"We'll set Russia free!"

Anyone with a little common sense would realize it's an absurd idea, but with the cushion hiding a bomb in their minds, and their plan to attach it to the automobile the tsar will be traveling in, Clementine and Vladimir set to work.

41. The Boxes

The wind blows constantly in St. Petersburg; it rests only six days each year. Today is one of those days: there is no wind when the portrait of Anna Karenina wends its way to the museum.

The Winter Palace has sent the prince's dark-green Mercedes limousine to collect the latest addition to the imperial collection. Mikhailov, the painter's heir (the one who's in the ranks of the secret police), doesn't want the painting to travel unnoticed, and he's pulled some strings; he knows "that kerosene contraption," as the tsar calls it, is his majesty's favorite, and people will notice. The portrait of Anna Karenina will travel by car.

Mikhailov has circulated the rumor about the automobile's journey through St. Petersburg, altering it, or, if you prefer, taking some poetic license. "A treasure for the tsar will be transported by Prince Orlov's automobile today. . . ." To spread the news, he plants it in a variety of circles and feeds it to a journalist who always has time for him; he knows he'll be intrigued— though Mikhailov suspects he won't be interested in the portrait itself. He always provides some facts, practically writing the articles for him, but this one he's embellished to ensure his interest.

So the journalist heads out in hot pursuit but is disappointed when he sees Prince Orlov is not at the wheel, and there's no sign of the tsar either. He follows the vehicle anyway; since its cargo is precious to the tsar, perhaps there is something there for his piece.

• • •

The museum carpenters have made a bespoke wooden box to the exact measurements of the painting. It has guide rails inside where the edges of the frame will slide in, so the canvas won't so much as graze the polished sides of the box, which are lined with thick felt.

The limousine stops in front of Sergei and Claudia's home. The sky is blue. The employees of the Hermitage Museum and the palace who were awaiting its arrival quickly gather around. The neighbors' servant comes out to see what's going on, and a few passersby pause to look; the curtains of adjacent windows flutter, hiding more discreet observers. The journalist watches all this from a distance.

The box is unloaded. The chauffeur will wait by the front door until the box is brought back out, portrait ensconced inside. The journalist thinks, *A gift for the Karenins from the tsar? There's no story here, not for me,* and departs in search of a better one; this time, his friend Mikhailov has failed him.

Giorgi jokes with one of the footmen from the Winter Palace. The footman's sister is a knockout. Giorgi wants to get on his good side because he has his eye on the girl and thinks he can approach her through him. But the chauffeur (whose stomach problems have put him in a foul mood) rains on his parade:

"Giorgi, you knew Aleksandra, didn't you?"

Although there's not a single cloud in the sky, a shadow descends on them.

"Answer me. Did you know her or not? If you did, tell me what the deuce she was doing with those troublemakers."

The nonexistent cloud hanging over their heads becomes denser, grayer, darker, a storm cloud. To Giorgi and the foot-man, the demonstrators aren't troublemakers. The footman believes that it was a religious procession—innocent, working-class fervor. Giorgi knows more, and he sympathizes with the demonstrators-turned-rebels—but not enough to have joined one of the cells. The grumpy Mercedes chauffeur is insistent.

"The tsar said someone with bad intentions stirred up the workers, there's no doubt about it. But tell me what Aleksandra was doing there? Why'd she go and get mixed up with—"

The footman interrupts. "Shut up. You know why, it was her brother. . . . You've heard the story a thousand times."

Silence. The limousine chauffeur wracks his small brain for something to say. There's no wind; he's at a loss for words. The horses on Nevsky break the silence; their hooves sound like ice cracking.

It's these hooves, all the more noticeable for the sudden lull in conversation, that awaken Claudia. Up in Sergei's room, she doesn't hear the box being brought inside or the footsteps of the servants carrying it so carefully or the difficulty they have turning the corner in the hall to the study. Giorgi's small talk (he hasn't stopped chattering since he returned from taking Sergei to the train station) was like a lullaby, so soothing that not even the sound of the Mercedes's motor awoke her.

Sergei didn't wake her up; he left early for Moscow to attend to a personal matter that enrages him, one of the many loose ends left by his uncle Stiva (Prince Oblonski) that concern him because they affect his inheritance. He's attending to this specific (and tedious) one today because it's an excuse not to be at home; he hasn't set eyes on the portrait of Anna Karenina since that time he saw it in front of his house, and he has no intention to either.

Unusually, Claudia has slept late. And she's surprised to find herself in Sergei's bed. Suddenly she remembers she brought Anna's manuscript upstairs. She makes a decision before jumping out of bed, and unusually, without dressing, she sits down at the desk and writes. Carefully, she composes a letter to the director of the Hermitage.

Dear Ivan Vsevolozhsky, we have decided to include, along with the portrait, two books. . . .

Here Claudia hesitates. "If I say two books, is that more confusing?" She decides to and starts over.

Dear Ivan Vsevolozhsky, we have decided to include, along with the portrait, the book Anna Karenina wrote. It will be of great interest to you because it is, in a way, another portrait of her. We don't expect any financial compensation for it. We ask only that you keep the manuscript confidential for fifty years, at which time the heads of the tsar's collection will decide whether or not to make it known and publish it, if they think it wise.

You will recall that, in its time, authorities judged it to be of excellent quality. We believe that the enclosed novel proves them correct.

Here Claudia pauses again. "Is this appropriate? Should I include a description of the novel?" She decides not to and continues writing.

Our sole intention is to leave it in safe custody to enrich the understanding and study of Mikhailov's accompanying portrait. If the museum sees fit to donate it to some other institution, you have our permission, the only condition is that it's not made public for the next fifty years. With our very highest regards . . .

Claudia prints Sergei's signature at the bottom of the page, forging it, and then her own, making it look timid. Then she writes another note to the curator of the museum.

Dear Ernest, we've decided to make a last-minute donation. We're including it with the painting. It's Anna Karenina's book. The blue box actually contains two books, two different versions. We've asked for a fifty-year embargo. If for some reason you can't accept this condition, we would like to have it back immediately, no negotiations.

This note also appears to be signed by them both. And it has a postscript.

I'd be most grateful if you would not mention the subject to my husband. I'm sure you can understand how difficult it is for him to speak any words at all (they are, after all, one's soul) about his mother.

She signs it without affectation, an honest signature with her characteristic decisiveness.

Claudia rings the service bell. With the help of the efficient maid, she's ready in no time. She speaks with her husband's undersecretary, Priteshko, entrusting him with the job of delivering her two letters and the blue box to the representatives of the museum.

"Madame, they've brought a motorcar to collect the painting, Prince Orlov's Mercedes."

"Mercedes?"

"It's the name of an automobile . . . that kerosene thing."

"Who's driving it?" The first thing that crosses her mind is an image of Prince Orlov; if Vlady is there, she should go out and greet him; he's one of the wealthiest, most powerful aristocrats, and he's always at the wheel if the tsar's aboard, out of concern for his safety; for him, it's a question of honor.

"A chauffeur, madame."

42. Anya Karenina

Anya is deeply chagrined by the donation of the portrait of
Anna Karenina. She doesn't remember her mother, despite trying hard to find a picture of her in her memory. She can remember her wet nurse clearly, as well as Sergei, whom she adored
throughout her childhood. The sale of the portrait shouldn't
upset her, but for Anya, it's her brother's worst betrayal.

"Why? Why is it doing this to me? Why do I feel this way?
What does it matter? I didn't even know the woman! But she's
my mother. Why . . . ? It shouldn't matter to me!"

She's in a terrible state of mind. She rings the bell for Valeria
to distract herself. She can't bear to go out—she knows today is
the day the portrait will be collected; she has no desire whatsoever to run into the cortege.

"Valeria, come talk to me. Tell me about your husband."

"He's on the submarine Potemkin, under the sea."

"I should be so lucky!"

"I wouldn't think so. They feed them rotten meat, it's
revolting."

"How do you know that?"

Valeria blushes when she answers.

"The telegraphist sends me messages."

"Oh! Why are you blushing, Valeria. Is he very handsome?"

"Not like my Matyushenko!"

"And why is the telegraphist writing you?"

Valeria turns red again.

"I can't tell you that, mademoiselle."

"Oh, all right, let's change the subject. Shall I teach you some
more French words today?"

Anya sighs. She really would like to be under the sea. She recites three words in French, but they sound wrong, unintelligible. Anya just can't concentrate on anything.

"Would it be all right with you, mademoiselle, if we got out the embroidery?"

Valeria sets down the sewing box, full of colored thread, buttons, pieces of lace. Anya's eyes flit from one to another. Her gaze loses focus. Anya thinks, *I want to be someone else, I want to be someone else.* In her mind's eye, she sees an underwater landscape—a forest of coral, caves, a giant pearl, a whale, a terrifying squid. . . . The contents of the sewing box evoke a whole Vernean world.

43. The Wind

So the wind is not blowing. Inside the palace car, Piotr holds the blue box and the letters under his left arm while he steadies a corner of the grand case that protects the portrait of Anna Karenina with his right. The Karenins' carriage follows thirty feet behind, Giorgi at the reins, the assistant curator of the Hermitage and Sergei's personal secretary, Priteshko, inside.

Piotr is singing. It's the first time he's traveled in a motorcar. He's so excited he invents a little ditty:

> With Anna, with Anna
> With Anna Karenina,
> Flying, flying
> In a Mercedes
> With Anna, with Anna.

On Nevsky Prospekt, a woman dressed in a pretty, heavy pink dress made of velvet and lace crosses the avenue, causing the grumpy chauffeur to brake suddenly. He shouts at the top of his lungs:

"Stupid cow! Are you drunk? Why are you crossing without looking? I nearly hit you! That's why you're poor—you're idiots!"

The woman is unperturbed. She wears a shawl of colorful flowers over her head; her long, shiny hair is loose. She moves slowly, crossing the street at an angle.

"Get a move on, you cretin!" the impatient, ill-humored chauffeur urges her. The motor rumbles, but the car can't advance. "Go ahead, take your time!"

Piotr keeps singing:

I'm in a Mercedes, I'm flying,
at Anna Karenina's side. . . .

Giorgi also comes to a sudden halt, keeping his distance. Up ahead, a young man with his back to him crosses the avenue at an angle, just like the woman who is shuffling in front of the Mercedes, but more decisively. When he's next to Orlov's car, he reverently places something on its rear bumper. He stops beside the car, takes two steps back, and bows respectfully.

Giorgi moves the carriage forward a few yards to see what the young man has left there—what's this about? It's a large cushion, embroidered with the words "Our Father."

"Hopeless," he thinks. "They still believe in 'their father.' The tsar condemns them to lives of misery, slaughters them in cold blood, and in return they honor him with gifts. Fools! They adore their oppressor!"

He holds the reins tightly. The car's motor will roar when it begins to move forward again at any moment now, and he doesn't want the horses to rear. He keeps his eye on them.

He can hear Piotr singing:

I'm flying along in an automobile,
dancing with Anna Karenina. . . .

At last the woman allows the Mercedes to proceed.

The chauffeur insults her once more as he passes.

"Laggard! That's why you're so poor!"

The fact that the wind's not blowing makes no difference to Giorgi or any of the pedestrians up and down the Nevsky, and despite the lack of wind, the odds are that Clementine and Vladimir's latest plot has failed. But thanks to that fact, the fuse the two anarchists have lit doesn't blow out, burning the trail to the bomb they have planted on the bumper.

Prince Orlov's green Mercedes, adorned with the handsome cushion at is rear, begins to move again. The sound of the motor startles the horses; Giorgi tightens the reins to control them. Out of the corner of his eye, he sees the young man who left the cushion begin to run away from the moving car. *Strange*, he thinks, *he's dressed like . . . could it be Vladimir?* Ahead of him— "Clementine!" Giorgi says. The woman dressed in pink is also running away from the automobile.

That's when the bomb explodes. The horses pulling the Karenins' carriage rear, frightened by the noise. Giorgi struggles to control them.

The attack that destroyed the Mercedes claimed six victims: the grumpy limousine chauffeur, Piotr (the singing footman), the woman who crossed the street to delay the car (Clementine), the young man who attached the cushion to the bumper (Vladimir), and two boxes inside the limousine—the newly built wooden one with the portrait of Anna Karenina inside, and the blue one with its silk ribbon, containing Anna's book and her other manuscript. The attack injured eleven people. One of the Karenins' carriage horses had to be put down. Giorgi can't understand how he came away unscathed.

The dress made in Paris, the one that Anna wore to the theater, dazzling everyone, was turned to bloodied rags by the explosion, but it was washed and mended by some of Clementine's erstwhile comrades. She was buried in it, in a mass grave, next to her beloved Vladimir, whose suit was also washed and mended, though we never had time to tell its story.

Coffee House Press began as a small letterpress operation in 1972 and has grown into an internationally renowned non-profit publisher of literary fiction, essay, poetry, and other work that doesn't fit neatly into genre categories.

Coffee House is both a publisher and an arts organization. Through our *Books in Action* program and publications, we've become interdisciplinary collaborators and incubators for new work and audience experiences. Our vision for the future is one where a publisher is a catalyst and connector.

LITERATURE
is not the same thing as
PUBLISHING

FUNDER ACKNOWLEDGMENTS

Coffee House Press is an internationally renowned independent book publisher and arts nonprofit based in Minneapolis, MN; through its literary publications and *Books in Action* program, Coffee House acts as a catalyst and connector—between authors and readers, ideas and resources, creativity and community, inspiration and action.

Coffee House Press books are made possible through the generous support of grants and donations from corporations, state and federal grant programs, family foundations, and the many individuals who believe in the transformational power of literature. This activity is made possible by the voters of Minnesota through a Minnesota State Arts Board Operating Support grant, thanks to the legislative appropriation from the Arts and Cultural Heritage Fund. Coffee House also receives major operating support from the Amazon Literary Partnership, Jerome Foundation, McKnight Foundation, Target Foundation, and the National Endowment for the Arts (NEA). To find out more about how NEA grants impact individuals and communities, visit www.arts.gov.

Coffee House Press receives additional support from the Elmer L. & Eleanor J. Andersen Foundation; the David & Mary Anderson Family Foundation; Bookmobile; Dorsey & Whitney LLP; Foundation Technologies; Fredrikson & Byron, P.A.; the Fringe Foundation; Kenneth Koch Literary Estate; the Matching Grant Program Fund of the Minneapolis Foundation; Mr. Pancks' Fund in memory of Graham Kimpton; the Schwab Charitable Fund; Schwegman, Lundberg & Woessner, P.A.; the Silicon Valley Community Foundation; and the U.S. Bank Foundation.

THE PUBLISHER'S CIRCLE OF COFFEE HOUSE PRESS

Publisher's Circle members make significant contributions to Coffee House Press's annual giving campaign. Understanding that a strong financial base is necessary for the press to meet the challenges and opportunities that arise each year, this group plays a crucial part in the success of Coffee House's mission.

Recent Publisher's Circle members include many anonymous donors, Suzanne Allen, Patricia A. Beithon, the E. Thomas Binger & Rebecca Rand Fund of the Minneapolis Foundation, Andrew Brantingham, Robert & Gail Buuck, Dave & Kelli Cloutier, Louise Copeland, Jane Dalrymple-Hollo & Stephen Parlato, Mary Ebert & Paul Stembler, Kaywin Feldman & Jim Lutz, Chris Fischbach & Katie Dublinski, Sally French, Jocelyn Hale & Glenn Miller, the Rehael Fund-Roger Hale/Nor Hall of the Minneapolis Foundation, Randy Hartten & Ron Lotz, Dylan Hicks & Nina Hale, William Hardacker, Randall Heath, Jeffrey Hom, Carl & Heidi Horsch, the Amy L. Hubbard & Geoffrey J. Kehoe Fund, Kenneth & Susan Kahn, Stephen & Isabel Keating, Julia Klein, the Kenneth Koch Literary Estate, Cinda Kornblum, Jennifer Kwon Dobbs & Stefan Liess, the Lambert Family Foundation, the Lenfestey Family Foundation, Joy Linsday Crow, Sarah Lutman & Rob Rudolph, the Carol & Aaron Mack Charitable Fund of the Minneapolis Foundation, George & Olga Mack, Joshua Mack & Ron Warren, Gillian McCain, Malcolm S. McDermid & Katie Windle, Mary & Malcolm McDermid, Sjur Midness & Briar Andresen, Daniel N. Smith III & Maureen Millea Smith, Peter Nelson & Jennifer Swenson, Enrique & Jennifer Olivarez, Alan Polsky, Marc Porter & James Hennessy, Robin Preble, Alexis Scott, Ruth Stricker Dayton, Jeffrey Sugerman & Sarah Schultz, Nan G. Swid, Kenneth Thorp in memory of Allan Kornblum & Rochelle Ratner, Patricia Tilton, Joanne Von Blon, Stu Wilson & Melissa Barker, Warren D. Woessner & Iris C. Freeman, and Margaret Wurtele.

For more information about the Publisher's Circle and other ways to support Coffee House Press books, authors, and activities, please visit www.coffeehousepress.org/pages/support or contact us at info@coffeehousepress.org.

Carmen Boullosa—a Cullman Center, a Guggenheim, a Deutscher Akademischer Austauschdienst, and a Fondo Nacional para la Cultura y las Artes Fellow—was born in Mexico City in 1954. She's a poet, playwright, essayist, novelist, and artist, and has been a professor at New York University; Columbia University; City College, City University of New York; Georgetown; and other institutions. She's now at Macaulay Honors College, City University of New York. The New York Public Library acquired her papers and artist books. More than a dozen books and over ninety dissertations have been written about her work.

Samantha Schnee is the founding editor of *Words Without Borders*, dedicated to publishing the world's best literature translated into English. Her translation of Boullosa's *Texas: The Great Theft* was longlisted for the International DUBLIN Literary Award and shortlisted for the PEN Translation Prize. She won the Gulf Coast Prize in Translation for her work on Boullosa's *El complot de los Románticos*.

The Book of Anna was designed by Bookmobile Design & Digital Publisher Services. Text is set in Marco Regular.